KAUAI TALES

P9-AGR-067

KAUAI

KAUAI TALES

Frederick B. Wichman

Illustrations by Christine Fayé

BAMBOO RIDGE PRESS
1985

Library of Congress Catalog Card Number: 85-61879
ISBN 0-910043-11-6

Third Printing, 1989

Text copyright ©1985 by Frederick B. Wichman
Illustrations copyright ©1985 by Christine Fayé

All rights reserved. This book, or parts hereof, may not be reproduced
in any form without permission of the author and /or illustrator.

Published by Bamboo Ridge Press
and the Hawaii Ethnic Resources Center: Talk Story, Inc.

Designed by Steve Shrader

Printed in the United States

This project has been supported in part by the State Foundation
on Culture and the Arts, the McInerny Foundation,
The G.N. Wilcox Trust, and the Frear Eleemosynary Trust

This is a special issue of
Bamboo Ridge, The Hawaii Writers' Quarterly.

Bamboo Ridge Press
P.O. Box 61781
Honolulu, Hawaii 96822-8781

CONTENTS

To Lorita Kuuleialoha
and Lisa Kamakakuokalani
with my love and thanks

PŌHAKU-O-KĀNE

CHRISTINE FAYE 1983

PŌHAKU-O-KĀNE

In the beginning before men and women came to Kauai, two brothers and their sister, traveling in the form of great rocks, rolled along the ocean floor seeking a home. They visited this atoll and that island but, not finding a place they liked, continued on their way.

In time they came to Kauai. Their path led upwards toward the surface of the sea. Speckles of sunlight flashed in the pale green water from a stream that washed over the weary travelers. The three slowed and stopped, letting the water wash off the salt that covered their rocky bodies. "This freshet brings life back to me," said the young sister. "I could stay here for a while."

"Not under the water, though," replied the first-born. "I want to feel the warmth of the sunlight on my back and the rain on my face. I want to be cooled by the breezes that come from the ocean by day and from the mountains at night. Let us go a little higher until we can look at the land. If it is a comfortable place, I shall climb up on shore and rest for a while. Come! Let us go into the sunlight."

He started out and his sister and brother followed. As they broke the calm surface of the sea, bright sunshine dazzled their eyes. Before them the waves rippled over a wide reef full of fish, eels, and lobsters. A green heron waded among the rocks while a tern splashed along the edge of the waves and a plover ran along the sandy beach chasing wary crabs.

The sister gazed at the reef, at the waves surging over it, breaking into white foam and spray, at the busy, noisy birds hunting the schools of brightly colored fish. It was a place, she felt, of endless fascination. "The reef! The reef!" murmured the sister happily. "I shall rest there until my strength comes back."

"Sister," said the eldest, "there on the reef the crabs will crawl over you and the tapering eel will hide beneath you. The red and green sea weeds will cover you and the birds will stand on your back to hunt the fish. This is not a restful place. Come with me to the mountain top, where there's a view over the land and ocean. We will see everything that happens below us. The clouds and soaring birds will bring us news from beyond the horizon."

"No, Brother," she interrupted. "Go to your mountain peak. Be shoved by every raging wind and be washed by each cold rain. I'll remain on the reef, lulled to sleep by the waves, and the crabs and birds and eels and fish will keep me company." The sister rolled out of the ocean and came to rest on the reef. She slept, warmed by the sunlight, cooled by the water. In this way, Oʻo-aʻa came to Hāʻena.

The brothers left their sister and rolled up the vine-covered sand dune. Just beyond the reach of stormy waves was a small grove of hala trees, their leaves casting a cool shadow in the hot afternoon. Here the younger brother stopped and refused to go any farther. "I am very tired," he said. "Here the earth is solid and the trade wind blows from the sea and rustles the leaves, a sound I like."

"Brother," replied the oldest-born, "listen to me. This is no place to rest. Vines will creep over you and cover you from sight. Lizards will crawl on you as rats burrow under you. The thorny hala leaves, as they fall, will scratch and hurt you. Come with me to the mountain top."

"No, I do not want to be way up there," answered the younger-born. "I would get dizzy and fall. I want to be with these trees and flowers and grasses that bend beneath the cooling wind. I prefer to sleep in this hala grove, lulled to sleep by the rustling leaves."

The second-born sank comfortably beneath the hala trees and drowsed. The soft wind chattered in the leaves and the ocean's roar gave him a feeling of peace. He called out once to Oʻo-aʻa but she was already asleep on the reef. The long rock slept. In this way Pōhaku-loa came to Hāʻena.

The land reared upward steeper and steeper until it reached a high point on a razor-sharp ridge that poured down from the mountains beyond. Alone, the oldest brother continued his climb. The ground grew steeper and steeper. There were no resting places for him and it took all his strength to climb higher. He reached the place where the steep cliff began, all that remained between him and his goal. One last effort and he would reach the peak. He tried, but his breath was coming in short, hot gasps and his vision was blurring. He was tired and for a moment he faltered. He tried to catch himself but he began to slip. Faster and faster he rolled back down the mountain.

He rested and planned a different route up to the peak. He climbed again until his strength was gone, rolled back, rested, and tried again. Days went by. It never occurred to him to give up, to return to sleep near his brother and sister. He wanted to reach that peak and he would rest only when he got there. He started out to climb again after every fall back to the bottom.

Kāne, the greatest of the gods, looking out over his lands, saw the rock struggling against a force greater than the rock could overcome. Kāne knew the first-born rock could never climb up that cliff to the peak. The way was too steep, the living rock too round. Nevertheless, Kāne saw that the rock would never give up trying to reach the peak. He admired this perseverance and wanted to know why the rock was so determined to reach that peak.

So Kāne went to the cliff at Hā'ena and stood beside the rock as the rock rested once again at the bottom of the climb. "You've tried to climb that cliff more times than seems reasonable," the great god said.

"And I will try again," replied the rock, "until I get to the top."

This was not an idle boast, Kāne realized. This rock would climb either until he did reach the top or until he had ground himself away into dust.

"Why?" asked the god. "Your brother and sister rest far below you. Why not return and join them?"

"From that peak, I can watch the birds and clouds of the sky and feel the winds blow and the rains washing over me. From there I can observe the trees grow and the plants flower and watch the whales and turtles glide by in the ocean."

Kāne laughed. "How will you watch so much if you are asleep like your brother and sister?"

"I will watch, not sleep," said the rock. He gathered his strength to attack the perpendicular cliff that stood between him and his heart's desire.

The great god took up the rock in his hand and lifted him to the top of the peak and set him down gently. "When I come again," Kāne said, "you must tell me what you have seen. When you are ready to go, the island will sink beneath the waters and the waves will climb up to you. Then you and your brother and sister may begin to travel again. Until then, watch and remember!"

The god disappeared as a mist blown by the breeze wavers and is gone, and the rock remained alone on the peak. Below him lay the grassy plains of Hā'ena and the dunes and beaches and the great ocean itself. The sun beat down on him and sometimes clouds cast their shadows over him. Curious seabirds soared past to look at him. Far below, Pōhaku-loa slept under the hala trees and O'o-a'a slept on the reef. There was much to be seen and to remember and the rock stored up many things to tell Kāne when Kāne came again.

In this way, Pōhaku-o-Kāne came to Hā'ena.

KANAKA-NUNUI-MOE

A long time ago, there was a giant living in Kawaihau among the low hills behind Kapaʻa town. He was so tall he could see above the coconut trees. If he sat very still, it was easy to mistake him for one of the hills. Anyone who did not know him was afraid of his great size, fearing the damage he might cause. However the people of Kawaihau loved him, for he was very friendly and went out of his way to be useful.

This giant was always careful where he stepped so that he would not injure anyone and he never destroyed taro patches or houses with a careless foot. When he wished to rest, he sat on one of the small hills above Kapaʻa. The villagers were glad when this happened for his weight flattened the hilltop, making another plot of ground fit for cultivation.

"He is very helpful," the Kapaʻa people said to astonished strangers who came to their land. "He does many things for us quickly that otherwise we could not do in many months."

Wherever this giant stepped he left deep footprints and in these deep holes the people planted banana trees. The villagers threw leaves, taro peelings, and other vegetable rubbish into these holes. When a compost had been formed, they planted banana sprouts. In this way, the people of Kapaʻa always had ripe bananas to give to the giant, for banana was his favorite food.

The giant yawned very often, for he was always sleepy. The gust of wind from his mouth often knocked down houses and blew the grass thatch into the sea. The giant was always very apologetic whenever this happened and he quickly brought logs from the uplands to rebuild the fallen houses and gathered pili for the thatching.

He found it difficult to stay awake more than a hundred years at a time. When he could no longer fight against the drowsiness overpowering him, he would sleep using a small hill for a pillow. Because of this, the people called him Kanaka-nunui-moe, the sleeping giant.

When he slept, Nunui slept for hundreds of years while the winds blew dirt over him and seeds were dropped there by the birds. The gentle showers sent by Ka-hale-lehua, goddess of the gentle rains, fed these seeds and a forest grew up over the giant. When Nunui awoke and stretched, the people of Kapaʻa fled in great fear, for what they had thought to be a hill had come alive.

One time, while Nunui was still awake, the high chief of Kawaihau wanted to build a large heiau to honor one of his gods. This was to be no ordinary temple. The chief wanted water-polished rocks for the walls and hard koa wood from Kōkeʻe for the framework of the god's house.

So the chief told the Kawaihau people what he wanted them to do. They must gather rocks from the golden brown waters of the Kōkeʻe streams and cut koa trees on the edges of Waimea canyon, and gather pili grass that grew at Mānā. "All this must be done in the turn of one moon," he ordered.

The unhappy people left their chief and silently returned to their village. The giant Nunui, stepping carefully among them, saw the long faces of the people. "What is wrong?" he asked.

The Kapaʻa villagers told him what they must do within the impossibly short time. "This cannot be done," the people said in low, sad voices. "How can we go to Kōkeʻe and bring back stones enough to build the walls in that time? And cut down the koa trees and bring the logs here and build the sacred house? And even if we do these things, who will cultivate our fields?"

Nunui smiled gently. "Tend to your fields," he said. "This work is nothing for me, and I'll gladly help you. Besides, it will give me something to do."

The giant went to Kōkeʻe and scooped up smooth, round boulders from the golden brown waters and brought them to Kapaʻa. "Chief," he called to the astonished ruler, "show me where you wish to build this heiau."

The amazed chief pointed out the place set aside for the temple. Nunui placed the rocks to form a wall, fitting them so closely together that not even a mouse could squeeze between the cracks. Within a week, he had built a strong, thick, handsome wall around the sacred place.

Nunui returned to the edge of Waimea canyon and cut down koa trees and trimmed them into the shapes he needed. He carried these back and made the framework of the house. He gathered pili grass from Mānā and wrapped the stems into bundles, tied these bundles to the framework, and within half the time the chief had set, the heiau was finished.

Everyone was happy. The farmers had been able to keep up with their chores, the chief had his heiau, and Nunui had something to do. There was even time enough for a celebration. The chief ordered all his people to gather bananas and to pound sweet potatoes and taro into poi. Some people hurried to slaughter pigs and dogs to be cooked in an imu, while others paddled out to sea to fill their canoes with fish and sent their wives to gather seaweed and 'opihi from the reef. At last, enough food for everyone was ready, and the chief, the villagers, and Nunui sat down before the overflowing bowls and platters.

"Eat," said the chief to Nunui. "After the work you have done, you must be hungry."

The giant ate all the food that had been put before him. When he was through, his stomach bulged and he was very sleepy. He chose a comfortable hill just a short distance above Kapa'a town. Nunui stretched a last time, lay down along the top of the hill, and soon was sound asleep.

As he slept through the years, the winds blew dirt over him and the birds brought seeds. Ka-hale-lehua, goddess of the gentle rains, sent showers to water the plants that now covered the giant.

So Kanaka-nunui-moe sleeps and sleeps and has come to resemble a long hill with a lump at one end where his nose is and a lump at the other end where his feet are. He no longer looks like a living being, but one day, perhaps soon, his eyes will open, he'll yawn and stretch his arms, and sit up.

NĀ PILIWALE

NĀ PILIWALE

The four Piliwale sisters were always hungry. They were thin and gaunt, emaciated by hunger. Each bone of their bodies could be plainly seen under the layers of wrinkled skin. Their fleshless hands resembled the claws of the bats that sleep by day. These women belonged to no chief who could care for them and so they wandered from island to island, to any place where the food was plentiful. There the sisters would stay, eating all that was at hand and grumbling loudly if their food was delayed in coming. They ate throughout the night and slept by day, for these four sisters belonged to those whom the sun's rays would turn to stone. In time their unwilling hosts would grow alarmed, for the food supply grew thin and disappeared and only then would they have some idea of how hungry the Piliwale sisters were.

The four sisters, when they were young, had argued in loud, bitter voices as to which one of them was the hungriest. They argued so long that all their food supplies ran out completely. Every valley, mountain ridge, plain, and reef around them had been stripped bare. There was no food left to bring the greedy sisters. The four sisters looked at each other in alarm.

"We are foolish," the oldest sister said. "We have argued so long that we are starving. It is one thing to be hungry, but quite another to be starving. We must have the priest of this place tell us which one of us is the most hungry." This was agreeable to all and they sent for a priest.

He hardly had need to consider the matter. "I have observed you four since you came," he told them. "Fish for fish, 'opihi for 'opihi, taro root for taro root, you have all eaten the same amount. Even if one shrimp remains, you cut it into four pieces and share it. Hungry? You are all equally hungry."

The Piliwale sisters were pleased with his answer and left that place and never returned. They never again argued as to which had the greatest appetite. Their stomachs were all equally distended and their belches were equally loud, scaring the same number of birds from resting places in the mountains. Although the sisters' faces were gaunt, their mouths were large and their teeth in excellent shape. The four sisters all consumed huge quantities of food and so quickly wore out the hospitality of their unwilling hosts.

Once, two of the sisters decided to visit the island of Kaua'i. Early one evening they landed their canoe on the beach of Kē'ē at Hā'ena. There the chief Lohiau, brother of Limaloa and Kahua-nui, came to greet them and, to their pleasure, called them by name.

"Welcome Piliwale-haluhalu!" Lohiau said to the eldest sister, and to the younger he said, "Welcome, Piliwale-kualana-ka-ōpū! You must be hungry after your long trip! One glance at you and I can see that! Come and eat your fill!"

Lohiau brought them to his home near the great hula school. There he seated them comfortably and ordered quantities of food to be set before his guests. They ate every bit of food brought to them. Finally they rose and, licking their fingers clean, went to join Lohiau where he awaited them.

"Never have I seen anyone eat as much!" Lohiau exclaimed. "Yet you still look starved to death."

"I always feel weak and fear I shall sink down into a faint," Haluhalu told him.

"You can see that my eyes are big with hunger," said Kualana. "I am always ready to eat."

"Is there any food that will stop your hunger for a while?" Lohiau asked.

"Only the fiddlehead of the hō'i'o," sighed Haluhalu, "with fresh shrimp from cold mountain streams."

"Mixed with a pinch of salt, and eaten like that, so crunchy between the teeth, so delectable to the tongue," sighed Kualana, wiping her chin.

Lohiau clasped his hands together in sorrow. "Oh, I am sorry, there is no hō'i'o to be found at Hā'ena. But great numbers of this fern grows in Kalalau. The hō'i'o is gathered by two families that live there. Perhaps if you went there you could eat your fill."

Eagerly, the two sisters thanked Lohiau and returned to their canoe for the journey along the cliffs of Nā-pali. Lohiau watched them go in relief. He was sorry for the two families about to offer hospitality to these gaunt women, but he needed time to make plans against their return.

As they landed on the night-shadowed beach of Kalalau, the two Piliwale sisters were pleased to see a fire flickering in the opening of a cave. Where there is a bonfire, they knew, there are people, and where there are people there is also food. The sisters climbed the path, shivering as the cool winds from Kōke'e caressed them. They reached the fire and held out their hands to the warmth.

The man and woman sitting by the fire looked sourly at the two scrawny women who had just appeared from the darkness. Then they looked away and ignored the Piliwale sisters. On the finely woven mats were bowls of food: poi, red seaweed, crushed roasted kukui nuts, bananas, and wild chickens. There was also a bowl of freshly picked hōʻiʻo and the eyes of the Piliwale sisters stared greedily at this.

The sisters stood, awaiting the invitation to sit and to help themselves from the bowls. No such invitation came. The couple by the fire never looked up as their fingers carried morsels of food to their mouths. Only the sounds of their greedy eating and the crackle of the fire reached the sisters' ears.

The sisters looked at each other, sharing their astonishment at such rude manners.

"Share your food with us," Haluhalu said, chiding the couple. "We are hungry."

"That is no concern of mine," said the man whose name was Kanaka-pīpine. With his free hand, he flipped a corner of the mat over the bowls of food.

"Give us at least a taste of hōʻiʻo," begged Kualana. "You have plenty of other food for you to eat."

"Be off with you!" Pīpine said, rising to his feet angrily. He seized a club and slapped it into his hand, a threat to back his order to move on. "I do not feed strangers who come begging at my fire. Where were you when it was time to prepare all this food? Gather your own hōʻiʻo. There is plenty in Kōkeʻe."

The Piliwale sisters were well aware that Kōkeʻe was thousands of feet above them and could only be reached by a steep trail that followed a sharp, thin ridge where the slightest misstep meant a fall to death. It was a dangerous climb at any time. Haluhalu's answer was mild.

"It is too dark to see the path," she said, "and we are too hungry."

"Try to beg some food from those people in there," Pīpine suggested. He gestured farther into the cave. The sisters peered into the darkness but could see nothing beyond the brightness of the fire. Kualana, whose eyes were always big, then made out faces reflecting the dim light. She saw hands motioning the sisters to come closer.

So the sisters left the fire and walked deeper into the cave. They came to a man and woman huddled together under a covering of tattered tapa, for the cave was damp and cold.

"How is it you have no fire?" asked Haluhalu. "It is cold here."

"Come wrap yourselves in our matting," the woman said. "We may share the warmth of our bodies. It is indeed cold here. I, He-wahine-manawale'a, and my husband, Ke-kāne-lokomaika'i, welcome you."

"Why don't you build a fire?" Haluhalu asked.

Ke-kāne explained, "If we were to build a fire, smoke would fill the cave and Pīpine would become angry. He would grab his club and beat us and make us put it out."

"This is a strange thing," muttered Kualana. "I never have encountered people so stingy and cruel." She glared angrily at the couple stretched out beside the warm fire at the cave entrance.

"I look at you," said Ke-kane, "and I can see you are hungry. You are welcome to share such food as we have, although it is not much and it is not cooked."

"You are kind and generous," Kualana said.

"Have you any hō'i'o?" Haluhalu asked. She, too, had noted the contrast in behavior, but there were more important things to think about at the moment.

"We do," Ke-kāne replied. "If that is your desire, you shall have it." He rose and brought bowls of food and placed them in front of the sisters. Then he went a little apart and sat with his back to them. It was forbidden for men and women to eat together, and in the small cave this was all the privacy he could give them. He prepared a special bowl for his guests, placing tender hō'i'o fiddleheads at the bottom of the calabash and arranging over them some fresh water shrimp sprinkled with red salt. He passed the bowl to his wife who placed it between the sisters.

"It is not much," He-wahine apologized. "We must give most of what we gather to that family by the fire in order to be allowed to use this part of the cave."

"We shall gather some more hō'i'o for you tomorrow," Ke-kāne promised.

The sisters slowly ate each 'opae and each fiddlehead with great enjoyment. Never had food been given them in such a generous manner. It sweetened the enjoyment.

"You have been very kind to strangers," Haluhalu said, "and the people in front have been very rude. You shall all be rewarded."

"We don't want a reward," Ke-kāne said. "We are glad to share what we have with you."

"Nevertheless," Haluhalu said, "listen to our words. Tomorrow take all you own and leave this cave."

"Where then would we live?" asked He-wahine. "There are no other caves in Kalalau."

"Leave that to us," Haluhalu said. "We will come again after the sun sets tomorrow. Remember! Leave this cave and take everything with you."

"We will remember," Ke-kāne said.

The Piliwale sisters left Ke-kāne and He-wahine to sleep through the night while they prowled the valley from one end to another. They found no caves in Kalalau and so they began to dig holes here and there searching for a good place to carve a cave until they came to the foot of a cliff where a stream flowed and kukui trees grew thickly. At dawn, the sisters stretched out on the floor of the new cave and fell asleep.

At dusk, they awoke and found Ke-kāne and He-wahine waiting for them. The couple was tired for they had spent the day gathering young hō'i'o fiddleheads and catching shrimp from the stream for the dinner of their guests. The sisters led them to the new cave and told them to build a fire and spread out their belongings and prepare the evening meal. Then the sisters returned to the fire of Pīpine.

"We are hungry," Haluhalu said. "Give us something to eat."

"I saw you eating last night," Pīpine said. "Eat with them again. There is no food for you here."

"So be it," the Piliwale sisters said. They left the cave, and stood facing it, their arms raised in prayer. Their emaciated figures swayed together as they chanted to the elemental forces they knew how to invoke. An avalanche of rocks fell from the roof of the cave, and the dust and noise filled Kalalau. The rocks and dirt covered the fire and the bowls of food and the soft mats and the bodies of stingy Kanaka-pīpine and his equally stingy wife.

"This is your reward for inhospitality!" the Piliwale sisters exclaimed.

Pleased with what they had done, they returned to the fire where their generous friends awaited them. There the sisters ate their fill of hōʻiʻo and ʻopae, lightly sprinkled with red salt. For once, they knew the pleasure of a full stomach and the lack of hunger.

"I like this place," Kualana sighed. "All of Nā-pali is beautiful and there is plenty of food."

Haluhalu replied, "Let us return to Hāʻena and join the retinue of Lohiau. We shall not go hungry again."

Meanwhile Lohiau and his sister Kahua-nui had been busy with plans of their own to greet these dangerous sisters upon the return of the sisters to Hāʻena.

So it was that the Piliwale sisters were pleased to find Lohiau waiting for them at Kēʻē beach. He entered their canoe and steered them to the beach where Mānoa stream crosses the sands. There the canoe was pulled up away from the waves and the sisters were conducted into a huge cave. Inside, where no rays of the sun could reach, the sisters found a sleeping house had been built for them. Deep piles of lau hala mats and tapa sheets were piled up to make comfortable beds and strands of maile and mokihana were hung from the rafters and perfumed the air.

"Sleep here," Lohiau told his pleased guests. "Tomorrow evening we shall gather together for a celebration of your arrival."

The sisters murmured to one another. "Truly, Lohiau is a great chief and lives in a land rich with food. Let's stay here for a long time."

That evening, they awoke to find Kahua-nui, chiefess of the hula school and sister of Lohiau, awaiting them. She led them to a pond nestled in the slopes below Pōhaku-o-Kāne that was fed by a gently flowing stream. When the sisters had bathed, Kahua-nui gave them clothes to wear of the softest tapa, intricately designed in a fiddlehead pattern. Leis of mokihana and maile were placed on their heads and around their shoulders.

"Never have we been treated with such hospitality!" exclaimed Haluhalu with deep contentment.

"Famed is the hospitality of Hāʻena!" Kualana said, quoting a proverb, her eyes bigger than ever with delight. "I look forward to a feast."

"Indeed, there will be much to eat later on," Kahua-nui assured them. "But first Lohiau and I have prepared a special program for your entertainment."

Kahua-nui led the Piliwale sisters farther up the valley and onto the ridge very near Pōhaku-o-Kāne. There a special platform had been built with a roof and three walls covered with matting to shelter the guests from wind and rain. Kahua-nui sat her guests facing the magnificent view of mountain and beach and grassy plain gleaming in the starlight. A bowl of 'awa was placed before each sister and was kept refilled throughout the long night.

Students from the hula school came to sing and dance the story of Ka-nē-loa and his search for the beautiful Ānuenue along the Waioli river. Before the sisters could express their hunger, food from the reef was offered them, sea urchins still alive in bowls of sea water, 'opihi fresh from the rocks and removed from their shells, red seaweed, sea cucumber, eel, squid, and lobster. More 'awa was poured and the sisters drank of it to ease their thirst as though it were water freshly taken from the spring of Waialoha.

Another story was chanted and danced, the adventures of Niu-lōlō-hiki, the mischievous coconut tree. Then food from the land was set before the sisters, pure white dog, purple lehua taro, banana, breadfruit, sugar cane. They ate steadily and drank and awaited the next entertainment with excited eyes.

Many dances later, many bowls of poi and 'awa consumed, the sisters began to yawn and move about in their places to stretch tired muscles.

"It's getting late," Kualana murmured.

"We should think of sleeping," her sister suggested, but she did not make the move to stand. She had never enjoyed herself so much and wondered what more Kahua-nui had to offer them.

Kahua-nui motioned to her servants who quickly cleared away all the empty bowls and replaced the soiled ti leaves. Then Kahua-nui said, "Honored guests, one last dish before you retire to sleep!"

The servants set before the sisters large heaps of hō'i'o, 'opae, and red salt. Greedily the Piliwale sisters ate, stuffing their mouths full.

They did not notice that Kahua-nui drew mats across the open wall, shutting off their view. They did not see the sky become pale and the white clouds blush as the first rays of the sun shone on the cliffs far above them. The sisters did not realize the platform had been built, not for the view, but to make it difficult for them to return quickly down the long ridge to their cave.

Then Kahua-nui ordered the mats around the house to be drawn away completely. "The morning air is refreshing," she said. "Let us greet the day!"

The Piliwale sisters looked up and leaped to their feet with wails of dismay.

"The sun!" shrieked one sister in fear. "I see the sun!"

"Run! Run for the cave!" called the other.

The sisters ran down the ridge as fast as they could, their gaunt legs stiff from sitting all night on the floor. Their heads were dizzy with the ʻawa and their stomachs were puffed out, so full of food they could not see their own feet. They ran, stumbled, fell, and stood to run again to reach the safety of their cave!

But Lohiau and Kahua-nui had planned too well. The sun rose above the mountain and its warm rays struck the sisters as they ran. With a last despairing wail, the Piliwale sisters turned to stone.

There they still stand as a warning to their other two sisters. Hāʻena is no place for a Piliwale to visit!

NIU-LŌLŌ-HIKI

NIU-LŌLŌ-HIKI

A long time ago, Ke-li'i-koa, high chief of Puna, was sleeping deeply. His hale moe lay near the mouth of Wailua beside the sacred grove of coconut trees. The wind from the mountains blew softly and did not disturb the coconut fronds. The waters of the wide Wailua chuckled happily, trickling over the sand-bar to mingle with the sea. The gentle ocean waves caressed the sands as little crabs danced lightly in the foam.

Outside the hale moe, hidden from view, were men who watched over the chief's sleeping. The nights at Wailua were calm and peaceful everywhere except where the chief slept. Night after night his sleep was rudely broken. There was some rascal, some kolohe fellow, who delighted in throwing coconuts through the chief's roof, waking him in sudden fright. Then as Ke-li'i-koa rushed from his house to catch the fellow, a coconut frond would fall just in front of him, tripping him and sending him sprawling in the dirt. After that the chief could not sleep and spent the rest of the night angrily watching the slow walk of the stars across the skies.

Before all this began, Ke-li'i-koa used to listen to his people's problems and perform all his chiefly duties before going to surf in the large waves. As the chief grew more and more tired from staying up all night, he began to sleep all day, stretched out on the sand dunes of Momo-iki. Then he did his duties only at night. The inhabitants of Puna grumbled for they were tired from working all day and were ready to rest.

"We can't sleep during the day!" they grumbled.

Ke-li'i-koa heard them and knew they were right. He had to sleep at night and work by day as everyone else did. So he ordered that guards should be posted around his hale moe to catch the rascally fellow who threw coconuts.

One of these guards, Kalukalu, was seated deep in the coconut grove where he could observe anything moving along the long rows of tall, straight tree trunks. He saw a rat scurry along the grass, searching for a fallen coconut to tear apart and eat. He watched an owl sweep low searching for the rat. He saw one of the coconut trees shake a little as though an earthquake had moved the ground. But no other tree had stirred and Kalukalu had not felt the earth move beneath him. The tree's fronds shook as though stretching as a child does when first awakening.

As Kalukalu watched in astonishment, the tree began to grow longer and taller until it could look out over the treetops around it. Taller and taller it grew, and, with little tremors that seemed caused by suppressed laughter, the tree leaned over its companions and continued to stretch out until it was bending over the sleeping form of chief Ke-li'i-koa. A coconut fell from the tree's crown and plunged through the grass roof, tearing open a large hole. The coconut burst open as it hit the floor and drenched the startled chief with its water. As he rushed from his hale moe with a roar of anger, a frond dropped in front of him, tangling his legs, and Ke-li'i-koa fell to the ground.

The giant tree swiftly shrank to its former size and soon could not be distinguished from any of the other trees in the grove. Kalukalu, rising from his hiding place, carefully marked the eight trees around this astonishing tree before hurrying to his angry chief.

Ke-li'i-koa was sitting up and pounding the ground with his fist. "Guards!" he bellowed. "Where is the kolohe fellow who dares to do this to me?"

"I saw no one," said the guard who had been watching along the river.

"Nor did I," said the man who had guarded the path down the ridge from the uplands.

"But I did," said Kalukalu and told the chief what he had seen.

Ke-li'i-koa listened and his anger grew. The tree had made his life miserable far too long. "Cut that coconut tree down," he ordered. "Cut it down and burn it so it can play no more tricks on me."

All the following day, woodcutters chopped at the tree. Great chunks of wood flew out and soon the ground was covered with chips of wood. The axes bit deep, knocking out a chip, but as soon as the axe was lifted away, fresh wood grew in again. For all the woodcutters' efforts, the coconut tree was not hurt. The pile of chips grew so deep that all the people who had come to watch took home wood for their fires that night.

That evening the rascally tree stood as it ever had and, as the chief tried to sleep, tossed down two coconuts to tease Ke-li'i-koa even more.

The next morning, Ke-li'i-koa asked Kalukalu, "What can I do against this tree? I cannot move from this place, for I must stay here at the source of my chiefly powers. The tree, it seems, cannot be cut down. What can I do? I must sleep."

Kalukalu replied, "Perhaps there is someone in Puna who knows how to cut down a tree like this."

"Perhaps," replied Ke-li'i-koa. "Therefore, send word throughout Puna. If there is any man who can cut this tree down, chop it into little pieces, and burn it, let him do so. In reward, he shall marry my daughter Kalili and rule after me."

Many men came to try to win the hand of the beautiful daughter of Ke-li'i-koa, high chief of Puna. They spent days chopping at the kolohe coconut tree as the people of Kapa'a cheered them on. Night after night, the bonfires burned brightly, fed by the chips of wood that lay thick on the ground. The tree stood firm and remained just as naughty and mischievous as it ever had been. Indeed, the tree grew more and more kolohe. Sometimes it would drop a coconut onto the head of an unwary axe-man, knocking him senseless to the ground. Sometimes the tree would not grow in fresh wood so quickly and would bend and sway as though it were about to fall. Then the people of Kapa'a would shout loudly. But the tree would straighten up again and there would be no sign of the chopper's hard work visible, and the people would groan in disappointment.

Far up the Wailua river in the uplands that touch the cliffs soaring to Wai-'ale'ale, a young man, Nā-lei-maile, lived with his grandmother, Nā-hale-maile. Vines of fragrant maile grew over their house, giving off a spicy scent in the drifting mists and soft rains. He was tall and strong, and fragments of the rainbow hovered about him as he moved along the misty uplands.

Nā-lei-maile heard the shouts followed by groans of disappointment echoing along the cliffs day after day. He asked, "What is that shouting, grandmother, that comes from the shore?"

"That noise is made by the people of Kapa'a," Nā-hale-maile answered. "Someone is trying to cut down a coconut tree and the spectators think it is about to fall and so shout their approval."

"There must be many coconut trees," the young man reasoned.

"Not so," his grandmother replied. "It is always the same tree."

Nā-lei-maile looked at his grandmother, his eyes asking the question tickling his tongue. Nā-hale-maile looked at her grandson both with admiration, for he had learned well the many lessons she had taught him, and with sadness, for it was now close to the time when he must leave her to lead his own life.

"This is no ordinary coconut tree," she told her grandson, "but a kupua, one of those beings who take several forms in their lives. Long ago, in the days now buried in fragments of men's memories, there was a hero named Maui who had eight brothers. Maui decided to join all of the islands of Hawai'i into one land. So he placed himself at the back of his canoe and set his brothers down to paddle it. Unknown to them, Maui brought on board their aunt, Hina-ke-ka'ā, for without her help he could not perform the task before him. But Maui warned his brothers never to look behind them no matter what they heard, for to do so would cause them to die. Maui let down his fishhook and caught Luehu, the great fish whose scaly humps are the islands of Hawai'i. Maui ordered his brothers to paddle for the shore. At first the canoe did not move, but the brothers were strong. Soon the canoe began to move and land began to rise from the waters. As the canoe neared the shore, the hordes of people who had gathered to watch began to shout, exclaiming at the beauty of the woman in the canoe.

"Completely surprised by this and ever curious, the eight brothers turned around to see who was in the canoe with them. Hina-ke-ka'ā dove into the sea to escape their astonished stares, and the fishing line broke, so the islands of Hawai'i were never joined together.

"In punishment, the brothers were turned to stone, except one, the eighth-born, for his magic was enough to change his form into a coconut tree. But this brother is very kolohe. He loves to play practical jokes, to tease and be mischievous. Nothing delights him more than to drop a coconut on the head of an unwary traveler or pour coconut milk on the hair of a woman passing by so she must go to the sea to bathe herself before setting out again on her journey. He has many tricks to discomfort others and amuse himself.

"And now the high chief of Puna, angry with all the tricks played upon him, has ordered the tree cut down. But of course, this tree is a kupua and cannot easily be felled, even if the prize of the man who can do it is the daughter of the high chief."

"I have seen the daughter of Chief Ke-li'i-koa," Nā-lei-maile said dreamily. "She is called Kalili after the soft, shy violet that grows at Wai'ale'ale. She is beautiful. I would like to make her my wife."

"She is of suitable rank for you," the young man's grandmother said, "and you for her."

"Grandmother, give me your permission to go and cut down this tree. I am strong!" The young man turned toward the sea, his heart already speeding along the downward path.

Nā-hale-maile smiled at her impetuous grandson. "Wait!" she counseled. "Wait until the tree grows more daring and more careless. Don't worry, you shall go, but not yet."

The young man heeded the words of his grandmother. He would never go without her permission for he had learned to respect her knowledge, her wisdom, and her advice, born of her many years of experience and learning. But in his heart he kept the picture of Kalili, the daughter of the high chief of Puna. Day after day he listened for the shouts of the Kapa'a people and heard their groans of disappointment and knew the tree still stood.

One day the shouts of the people grew very loud and lasted a long time. "Grandmother!" Nā-lei-maile called anxiously, "listen to the people! The tree is falling!"

"No, my grandson," Nā-hale-maile replied. "It grows more daring, that is all. It leans forward on its trunk, looking as though it were about to collapse at any moment, but it does not. It will straighten up again and be as strong and upright as ever."

Indeed, the groans of disappointment echoing along the cliffs proved it was so. The tree still stood.

"Let me go, grandmother," pleaded the young man.

With a sigh, Nā-hale-maile said, "Yes, it is time. But listen to my words carefully. Here is an axe. Chop at the trunk with clean strokes. As you cut at it, the tree will lean far over and sway and shake like the most experienced dancer to ever come from Hā'ena. It will tease you and try to drop coconuts on your head and knock you down with a falling frond and hit you with the chips you chop from its side. Dodge all these and you will not be hurt. Then the tree will lean far, far over and his crown will touch the ground. When he does this, my grandson, take these leis of maile and throw them into the topmost fronds of the tree. The maile will root and hold this tree tight to the ground. As the tree struggles to regain its upright position, call it by name: Niu-lōlō-hiki. When you call a kupua by its true name, you control the forces within it. Then indeed the tree will fall and you may claim the chiefess Kalili in marriage."

Quickly Nā-lei-maile went down the path to the sea with many strands of maile draped across his shoulders and an axe held firmly in one hand. He came to the high chief of Puna and kneeled before him. Kalili stirred from her place and came to lean on her father's shoulders.

Nā-lei-maile looked at the chiefess and she smiled. He answered her smile and love filled their hearts.

"Great chief," Nā-lei-maile said, "give me permission to cut down this coconut tree. Let me give you nights of peace and sleep."

"Many have tried," answered the discouraged chief. "Many have failed."

"Let him try, father," Kalili urged. She smiled again at the young man kneeling before them. "Perhaps he who comes covered with maile leis from the misty uplands can do what others have failed to do."

"Let me try," the young man repeated eagerly. "At worst, I can only fail. At best, I shall win." He spoke to the chief but his eyes never left those of Kalili.

Ke-liʻi-koa nodded. "Go," he ordered. "Cut down this kolohe tree. Give me nights of peace and sleep."

The chiefess Kalili herself led Nā-lei-maile to the tree. The people of Kapaʻa gathered about to watch, knowing there would soon be many chips of wood to feed their bonfires.

Nā-lei-maile gripped his axe tightly and swung it. The axe cut deeply into the tree trunk. With a twist of the axe, the young man flicked out a large wood chip. The chip, aimed by the tree, changed direction and sped toward the maile-laden man. It came so fast it would have badly hurt Nā-lei-maile had it struck. But the young man dodged it with a laugh.

"I am not hurt so easily!" Nā-lei-maile called out.

He chopped again and again, dodging each of the chips until a huge mound of them were heaped all around the tree. A coconut, then another, plunged from the crown, but Nā-lei-maile dodged them easily. The kupua began to grow taller. The axe could never strike at the same place twice for the tree grew too quickly.

The rascally tree began to tease the young man and danced and swayed, leaning over farther and farther as though about to lose its balance and fall. The people of Kapaʻa shouted encouragement to the young man. The tree, enjoying the sounds, enjoying teasing, grew more daring yet. It leaned toward Kapaʻa and touched its leafy crown to the ground.

"It falls!" the people of Kapaʻa yelled in excitement. "The tree falls!"

But they groaned in disappointment the next moment, for the tree started to straighten up once again. The young man pulled the maile from his neck and tossed it into the kupua's crown. The maile fell over the trunk and anchored itself in the ground on either side. The tree struggled to right itself, but the maile, solidly anchored in the earth, held fast.

Nā-lei-maile, standing where the roots of the giant tree strained to upright the tree, called out, "Tree! I give you your name! You are Niu-lōlō-hiki, Maui's brother, who should have perished with your brothers! Join them now!"

The kupua, hearing its name, ceased struggling and Nā-lei-maile felt the force of the kupua drain away. He gave two more axe swings to the weakened trunk and the tree fell to the ground.

The people of Kapaʻa cheered and yelled with great enjoyment. They chopped the trunk into pieces to lug some home for their fires. They prepared a feast in honor of the marriage of Nā-lei-maile and Kalili.

From then on, Ke-liʻi-koa slept soundly in his house on the banks of the Wai-lua. He never again, however, went under a coconut tree, for all those coconuts Niu-lōlō-hiki had thrown at the woodcutters had sprouted and grown into trees. These trees, even now, drop coconuts and fronds on the heads of careless travelers.

MA-KA-IHU-WA‘A

Every night Menehune fishermen took their canoes from sheds under the hala trees and carried them across the beach at Hanalei. They launched their outrigger canoes and paddled swiftly across the bay and over the reef to the ocean beyond.

Once safely out to sea, some fishermen scattered west to Hā'ena or east to Kilauea to secret fishing grounds. Here they tossed overboard their weighted lines tied with many hooks. A good fisherman knew where the fish lived and what it ate and baited his hooks with the right foods. Leaving their lines firmly tied to a float, these off-shore fishermen moved from place to place. Here they dropped off other lines, each hook baited with cooked sweet potato, a favorite food of the 'opelu fish. There they caught squid by dancing a shiny cowry shell in the dark waters, a lure no squid could resist. Then the fishermen would return and gather up their lines. If the fisherman was skillful, every hook would hold a fish. At last these fishermen rode the waves into Hanalei bay and added their catch to the store of food that would feed all the Menehune at their daily feast that finished just before daybreak.

The deep-sea fleet searched for schools of fish which the fishermen caught in basket traps. They would dump basket after basket of glittering fish into their canoes until the canoes were so full they sank dangerously close to the water line. Often, following the schools of fish, the Menehune fleet would sail far out to sea where the fishermen could no longer see the dim outline of the island. Then they used the stars to guide them back to shore. They knew where the traveling stars were at any time of year, those stars, like Nā-holoholo that moved about the skies and appeared just before dawn in the east, warning the fishermen of the coming sun. The Menehune also used the fixed stars, like the seven stars of Nā-hiku that walked the same path night after night.

Even during cloudy nights the Menehune launched their canoes to fish. They were careful not to paddle so far out they could not find their way back. The clouds hid the stars and often hid the land from them.

But it was the stormy nights that were worst, those nights when the wind blew strongly, driving the waves like frightened birds in front of it. The rain would pour down in a never-ending sheet that hid the island from the Menehune. The wind-driven waves would climb taller and taller, sending the canoes on wild rides up and down those mountainous walls that seemed alive with all the dangerous demons of the ocean. There was no time to look for the land then. The fisherman had to concentrate on the waves to keep his canoe from swamping or from getting caught by a breaking wave that would upset the canoe and send it to the bottom. The waves and wind roared and only when it was almost too late the roar changed tone when the wave angrily smashed on the reef, and the fishermen had to paddle frantically to stand farther out to sea. In the middle of the waves, wind and rain, it was hard to remember how to find one's way back to shore, for there was nothing to be seen of the dark island. Yet the Menehune went out to catch what fish they could on such nights. There was never enough fish to satisfy the great appetites of the Menehune people.

After one such terrible night as the fishermen cleaned their meager catch, their chief came to visit them. Before him walked two men carrying torches. Behind him came two more torchbearers. The chief was still young, his beard bushy and brown, but he was wise. He saw the skimpy catch. He saw the frustration in his fishermen's eyes. He saw them shivering in the misty rain that still blew down from the cold mountains. He knew his fishermen were proud of their skills and of their cunning, proud to bring much food to the common table.

The chief gestured to the heavy clouds overhead, to the ocean muttering along the reef, to the canoes empty of fish. "A good catch, considering the night," he said.

One of the fishermen, an owl-eyed, bow-legged man who was afraid of no shark or man either for that matter, refused the kindly words.

"No, it isn't a good catch," he said boldly. "There's not enough fish for us all. We'll have to eat some dried fish tonight. We can't catch fish on such a night as this."

To mark his words, the rain goddess Ka-hale-lehua threw down a burst of heavy rain drops that put out one of the torches surrounding the chief. Its bearer attempted to relight his torch at another, but his clumsiness only managed to extinguish another torch.

"The night grows dim indeed," the chief joked, trying not to laugh at the antics of his torchbearers.

The owl-eyed fisherman had not finished. "The farther from shore, the darker the night. We can't go out to where the fish are. There is nothing to guide us back when the sky is covered with rain-filled clouds."

"That is the problem of these stormy nights," the chief agreed. "We must find a way for you to fish on cloudy nights. Or you must not go out at all."

The fishermen groaned at the suggestion that they not fish at all.

"I will think about this," the chief promised. "Perhaps the gods will help me find an answer."

Just then the rain goddess emptied her water bowls. Heavy, fat drops of water fell like a river directly from the sky to the earth. The remaining two torches that lit the chief's way went out.

"Like us," the fishermen laughed, "you must return home in the dark."

"Nevertheless, you have done well," the chief said, "to go out at all on such a night. Each mouthful will be more delicious because we know the courage it took to bring back even this much from the sea."

The fishermen cheered him and finished their chores with lighter spirits.

The chief strained his eyes to see the path on this dark, rainy night, and stumbled over roots and stones. His torchbearers followed him, tripping over vines, banging into branches, and stumbling over each other, trusting their chief to lead them back to safety again.

The rest of that night the chief thought deeply about his fishermen's problems. He understood their pride to provide enough fish to feed their friends and family. He understood that some nights were stormy. That is why he had, long ago, ordered that fish be dried and set aside under cover so that there would be seafood in times of need. He could simply order the men to stay ashore on stormy nights when the clouds covered the sky and most of the mountains, too. In that case, he would need something for them to do. The difficulty was that dark and stormy nights weren't very useful to anybody. Rain and wind made all work more difficult to do.

There was no question of waiting for daylight and returning to shore then. Sunlight was fatal to a Menehune. A ray of sunshine could turn him to stone instantly. There were many stones scattered over Kauai that had once been living people.

What about ropes? One canoe would stop while the land could still be seen. A rope would be tied to that canoe and passed to a second one which would paddle farther out, pass a new rope to a third canoe, and so on. No, the chief decided, that would not do either. The canoes would not be free to follow the fish. Windy and stormy nights brought large waves that would break the ropes. Would it even be possible for ropes to be made long enough and strong enough?

As darkness came again and the fishermen were gathering their nets and baiting their hooks, the chief still continued to think. The night was dark again and the clouds hid the stars and mountains. A lamakū was set ablaze and stuck in the sand beside the chief. A lamakū is made of strings of oily kukui nuts tied together with a twine made of dried banana leaves. Ten strings are woven around a short pole, forming a cylinder six inches across and four feet tall. The bottom kukui is set on fire and, like a candle, feeds on oil released by the heat. The flame slowly passes from nut to nut, giving off bright light and dense smoke.

The chief twisted the ends of his beard and stared at the lamakū with unfocused eyes. Suddenly his eyes widened and he began laughing, a deep booming laugh that brought his torchbearers eager to share in the joke. As the chief saw their puzzled faces, he laughed all the harder. He had suddenly realized that, even in the dark night, he could see. It was night. It was dark. The flames gave a light. Many lamakū would give a lot of light.

"There will be lights to guide our fishermen to shore," the chief told his torchbearers. "If we prepare a lot of lamakū, we can stick them in the sand. The fishermen will see the light and know where their landing place is."

The chief called all his people together who were not directly farming or gathering food. He ordered them—old women, old men, young mothers and younger children—to gather every kukui nut of the right size from the trees and to cut off leaves from banana plants and braid them into cord. Once these were gathered, the kukui nuts were shelled and woven into the cylinders that became lamakū. A lamakū burned for several hours, so in the early hours of the morning, the chief ordered all the lamakū that were ready to be placed on the beach and set afire.

The clouds still covered sky and mountain. Ka-hale-lehua was busy emptying out her water bowls. There was nothing to guide the fishermen back to shore except their own sense of direction and the changeable currents of the sea. But now there was also a line of lamakū burning and sputtering along the beach.

When the canoes returned before dawn, the chief was waiting beside the cluster of torches. Eagerly he questioned them, "Did this light help you?"

The fishermen nodded, but there was no outburst of enthusiasm, which the chief had expected. He looked at his fishermen one by one, his stern eye causing them to drop their heads and shuffle their feet in the sand.

At last the owl-eyed fisherman spoke up. "Chief," he said, "the light does help. A little. A very little. When we saw the light, we paddled farther out. But we still cannot go where the deep sea fish swim in great schools."

"That is too bad," the chief said, unhappy and discouraged.

The owl-eyed fisherman, who was afraid of no shark or man for that matter, spoke up again. "The idea is good. The lights are good. But they need to be higher."

"Higher?" asked the chief. "You mean, put the lamakū on top of the coconut trees?"

Everyone laughed at the silly idea. The coconut trees themselves would flame up in giant torches. In one night the trees would be lost. So would a supply of food.

"Higher than that," answered the fisherman, quite unworried that people were laughing at him. "Much higher than tree tops." He pointed his hand toward the west.

Everyone turned to look. They saw the beach, the line of coconut and hala trees, and beyond that there was the flat plain of Hanalei through which Waioli stream and Hanalei river cut meandering paths to the sea. Beyond that, there were the ridges that stretched taller and taller until they melted into the great mountains of Maunahihi and Nā-molokama. But most of the view beyond the trees was out of sight, behind clouds and mist and fog. Only the lowest ridge could be seen where it started up from the edge of Waioli stream.

The chief nodded, delighted with the suggestion made by his owl-eyed fisherman. "Yes, we shall place lamakū there on that ridge," he said. "Just below the clouds, far above the trees."

There was almost no time left before the sun would climb over the Anahola mountains, so the chief ordered the Menehune to finish up what chores they could and rest. He slept soundly that day, knowing the night would be a busy one.

Once again the night was stormy and dark. Clouds scudded low over Hanalei. The rain goddess sent a steady rain that the wind blew this way and that, as though pulling aside curtains to peer through a window at the busy Menehune. But the fishermen pushed out to sea with lighter hearts than usual. The chief ordered lamakū to be made and brought to him. With a crew of workers, including his torchbearers, he climbed up the ridge. When he could look out over the tree tops and the clouds swirled just above his head, the chief struck the ground with his heel. "Here we must dig out a platform from the edge of the ridge, large enough to place all the lamakū we need to light our fishermen home again."

The Menehune went about the chore with their usual good sense, sound engineering, and the knowledge that many hands working together make any chore easier and quicker. A small platform dug out of the side of a hill was a simple chore compared to many others they had done in years past. There was no trouble organizing work groups. One group dug away the dirt and formed the platform. Another group formed a line reaching to the river beds of Waipa'a and Waikoko and passed smooth stones hand to hand to the worksite. Before half the night was gone, the platform was finished and paved with the stones. All that time the torchbearers were busy trying to keep their torches lit. The wind was strong but the flames were stronger, enjoying their dance. However, the rain sometimes fell so hard that the flames sputtered and danced away so far they became lost and went out.

The chief sat farther up the ridge where he could see the work, and his voice shouting instructions could be heard. He listened to the songs that the workers sang as they worked. He laughed at his torchbearers as they ran here and there trying to relight their torches as their torches were put out by the goddess Kahale-lehua as she emptied out the water that always collected in her bowls. He laughed but he realized that the lamakū that would guide the fishermen would also be put out by the rain.

"Build a roof over the platform," he yelled into the stormy night. "It must be higher in front than in back. It must protect the torches from the rain. It must also be high enough so the roof won't catch on fire."

No sooner said than the work started. One group cut logs for the uprights and the roof frame. Another group went for banana leaves which, laid down carefully, made a waterproof cover. Soon a flat roof with no walls had been built over the platform. The lamakū were set in place and lit. For the rest of the night the flames sputtered and danced and poured a beacon of light into the dark and stormy night.

The canoes came swooping into shore on the backs of waves that threatened to swamp the small canoes that were so deeply filled with fish. As the owl-eyed fisherman lifted his paddle, all the fisherfolk gave a great cheer. "We have caught enough fish for two nights," the owl-eyed fisherman said. "With this light we can sail far out to sea and find our way back, no matter what the weather."

The Menehune lifted their chief onto their shoulders and paraded back to their eating house, cheering and laughing happily. The fishermen saw to it that the chief got the tastiest bits from their catch, those treats they usually held back for themselves or ate while still in the canoes. Just as delighted, the chief ordered that the next night would be spent in games and enjoyment.

That is how the Menehune invented a lighthouse. The platform they had made for the lamakū was named Ma-ka-ihu-wa'a, "At the canoe's prow." The platform is gone now, like the Menehune, but the ridge where it had been is still named Ma-ka-ihu-wa'a and the ridge still dips its toes into the happy waters of Waioli stream.

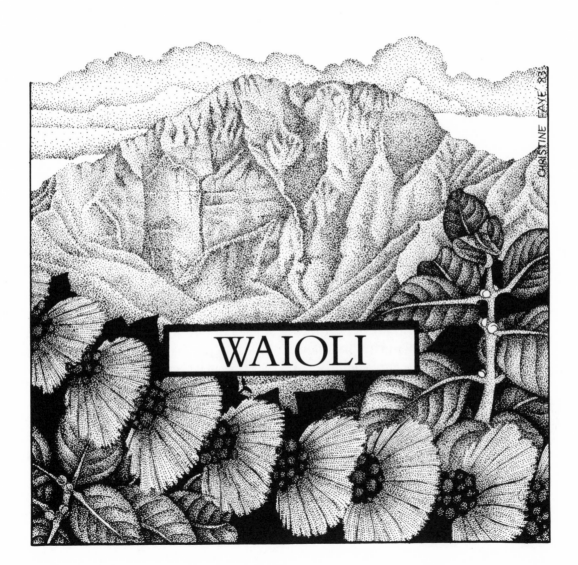

WAIOLI

WAIOLI

Ka-nē-loa was on the move. He sailed from island to island on his great double-hulled canoe seeking Waioli, the singing water. He had heard her song floating on the trade winds that blew over his native island far to the south, an echo on the whispering wind:

Kā-ne-loa!
Sleepless the nights I spend waiting
For you to come!
Only you can find the gifts
To win my love.
Kā-ne-loa, do you sleep?
Dare the unknown!
Seek the sister of the gods!
Search for me, Ka-nē-loa,
Hidden am I
Beside the singing water
Of Waioli!

Farther and farther north he came, following the fixed star of a new sky and using the fiery reflection of volcanoes as a beacon.

At last he stood on his deck looking at the curved bowl of Hanalei. A reef, stretching from headland to headland, protected the bay within. The waters lapped at a golden crescent beach. Beyond that was a flat, grassy plain surrounded on three sides by ridges that ran gently up to the feet of towering sheer-faced mountains. In the center was a massive cliff. Several waterfalls fell slowly down its face, the thin lines of water twisting and turning in the wind. From one of the cascades a stream wound down to the sea. It was not wide like the river that gave this valley its name, Hanalei, but the stream sang and chattered as it worked its way down to the shore.

Ka-nē-loa stood, waiting outside Hanalei bay. He had come upon an errand, following the voice of a woman he had never seen. Her voice came to him, floating against the wind down from the mountains:

Search for me, Ka-nē-loa!
Hidden am I
Beside the singing water
Of Waioli.

With a shout, Ka-nē-loa ordered his crew to dig their paddles deep into the sea. Like a great sea bird, the canoe sped across the reef into the calm waters of the bay.

As he floated past, a young woman beckoned to him from a canoe anchored to the reef. Her dark hair was tinted red by the sun and salt air. A circle of crimson feathers circled her head like a flame. The brilliant sun reflected from her salt-bleached tapa dress, on which was stamped a design of sea urchins. Their glowing color came from a dye made of noni bark which turned a lobster red when dipped in sea water. Around her neck was a double strand of tiny flame-colored shells.

"Come, Ka-nē-loa, I have been waiting for you!" she called. "Here where the waters of Waioli mix with the ocean."

Even though her skin was flushed to high color by the sun reflected from the waves, he could see that she blushed even as he came nearer.

Her manner, at once bold and shy, attracted him. Her voice was low and clear, like the resounding sea. Her eyes like sparkling flames drew him nearer to their warmth.

"I have come a long way to find a wife," he replied. "I am glad to find you waiting for me."

She glanced quickly at him and away. Her blushes flickered like a bonfire on a windy night. "Join me in my canoe," she said. "Here is a tapa sheet I have dyed red by dipping it in noni sap and into the ocean. Now its redness shall remind us of a warming fire as it covers us during the chilly night."

The air about them was warm, perfumed by seaweed and salt. The beach of white sand seemed as though the crescent moon had come here to rest beside the sparkling sea. A grassy plain flowed towards gigantic ridges of sheer cliffs. Down the center of the highest cliff a waterfall dropped lazily. In such a place, with such a woman, he could remain happily.

"What place is this?" he asked dreamily, more to hear her voice again than to learn a name.

"This is Mono-lau," she answered. "Here Waioli stream enters the ocean, a rich fertile place for the reef plants and animals. Here in these brackish waters, the canoes strain against their ropes, ready to begin their journey."

In that moment, Ka-nē-loa knew that this woman and this place were not for him. "I'm sorry," he said, "but I will not join you. I have already searched far and wide over the ocean. I am not going back to sea. You are not the woman I seek."

The woman of Mono-lau laughed. Was it happiness, relief, or was she mocking him? She stood up in her canoe. She quickly folded the tapa sheet of solid red, tied it tightly, and tossed it into his canoe.

"This is my gift for your future wife," she said.

The sun, reflecting from the waves, blinded him a moment. When he had blinked his eyes clear, the woman of Mono-lau was no longer there. Only her canoe remained bobbing gently up and down in the ripples. A breath of mountain wind puffed past Ka-nē-loa. It brought the perfume of mountains and valleys to mingle with the scents of ocean and shore. With this perfume came the echo of a woman's voice:

> Let my sister rest
> At Mono-lau!
> A gift she gives. Soft and warm
> Tapa, noni-stained, is yours.
> Nothing more do you need there.
> Ka-nē-loa, search for me!
> Look beside the singing stream
> Of Waioli!

Ka-nē-loa beached his canoe, picked up his tapa and crossed the wide crescent of sand. Here, a stream of fresh water was blocked by a ridge of sand from entering the bay. Behind this fragile dam, the water spread out, resting from its long journey across the valley. The pond could only grow larger and larger as more water flowed into it. The pressure of this water, Ka-nē-loa noted, in time would break the dam and the whole pond would drain into the sea. This was a resting place between two actions, a peaceful moment, a peaceful place.

Beside the pond there was a hau tree, covered with flowers, some of which had dropped onto the still surface of the water. They had faded but like all hau flowers, they became ever more resplendent, deepening into a color that mixed yellows and smoldering reds. There was a woman sitting against the tree trunk, a lei of red-yellow hau flowers and fern on her head. Around her lay tapa-making tools, the anvil and the beaters, over which rested a tapa sheet the same color as the fading flowers.

This woman beckoned to Ka-nē-loa and patted the ground beside her, inviting him to join her.

"Come, Ka-nē-loa," she called, "I have been waiting for you!"

Everything about this woman was restful. Her voice was low and melodious, soothing and calm. This was a woman who had worked hard and would work hard again, but now, at this moment, was resting placidly and peacefully. She was in balance, even to the color of the tapa which she was folding with slow movements of her hands, this color balanced between red and yellow, neither one nor the other, yet both. As he breathed deeply in contentment, he smelled a sweet yet sharp smell, reminding him of bogs and high mountains and shiny black seeds, the smell of 'alani wai.

"I have come a long way to find a wife," he said. "I am glad to find you waiting for me."

She smiled contentedly at Ka-nē-loa as a mother will smile at a favorite child. "Stay with me here," she murmured. "Here is a tapa sheet to cover us when the night grows cold. I have colored it yellow-red by adding the leaves of the 'alani. The 'alani also perfumes it."

The spicy scent of 'alani, more delicate than mokihana, lulled him. Hau flowers dropped silently on the still water of the pond and kissed their reflections in lazy contentment. The tree hid all else from view, no mountains loomed above, no ocean rocked behind. The world shrank into this one calm moment of fulfillment and promise.

"What place is this where I am content to stay?" Ka-nē-loa asked. To know this name seemed a precious thing to him in that moment.

"This is Māhā-mōkū," she told him. "Here the Waioli stream rests and dreams after its long journey down the valley. Here it rests, quiet, calm, yet swelling wider and deeper. A pond that remembers its past journey and reflects on what is to be, that is Māhā-mōkū."

Ka-nē-loa stood up. "I am sorry," he said, "but you are not the woman I am looking for, nor is this the place for me. I will not join you, for my journey is not yet over. It is not time for me to rest."

The woman of Māhā-mōkū rose to her feet like one who knows the resting time is over. With swift movements, she tied her tapa sheet into a bundle.

"This is my gift for your future wife," she said.

She threw the tapa straight at Ka-nē-loa. Surprised, his whole attention became centered on catching the bundle. When he looked up again, the woman and the pond were gone. The dam was breached and the waters ate at the sand, clearing a deeper and wider channel with each passing moment. The waters of Waioli rushed to greet the sea.

A breath of mountain wind puffed past Ka-nē-loa, bringing mountain scents to mingle with the sea smells and the perfumed 'alani. This same wind carried the echo of a song:

> Let my sister be
> Māhā-mōkū.
> A gift she gives. Tapa fragrant
> With 'alani wai is yours.
> Nothing more do you need there.
> Ka-nē-loa, search for me!
> Look beside the singing stream
> Of Waioli!

Ka-nē-loa continued to follow the east bank of the stream, the two tapa sheets cradled in his left hand. On his right the ridge of Ma-ka-ihu-wa'a dipped its toes in the water and angled upward toward the steep mountains. The sun was warm and the breeze cool. Ahead he could see a flat, grassy plain, dotted here and there with trees, and the broad, shiny ribbon cutting through it flowing around the hill that was once a dragon, Ka-moʻo-kōlea-ka, who, with a great show of friendliness it certainly didn't feel, lured unwary folk to their deaths.

Ka-nē-loa came upon a meander whose great broad loop began and ended only a few feet apart. The stream could burst through the dirt embankment if it chose and hurry seaward by a quicker route. Instead, the water seemed undecided whether to flow to the sea or return to the mountains, and so in a wide loop collected its thoughts tranquilly, the broad water a mirror of mountain and cloud, of sky and plain, all the colors of this place yellowed by the reflection from the muddy water.

As Ka-nē-loa stopped to admire the view, a gentle rain fell, each drop reflecting the soft yellow color of early dawn. The yellowish hue of the water intensified and everything became tinged with the soft yellow glow.

"This is Ua-lena, the yellow-tinted rain of Hanalei," a woman's voice said. "And you are at Lani-huli, where the high chief of the sky tries to persuade the stream to return to the mountains whence it came."

She was seated on a pale yellow reed mat on the peninsula formed by the indecisive water. Before her was a wooden anvil used for tapa making and across it lay a fine sheet of softest tapa dyed a brilliant light yellow by soaking it in a bath of raw ʻōlena root. Around her neck was a lei of maʻo-hau-hele, the yellow hibiscus. There was a lei of yellow feathers twined in her hair.

The woman spoke again. "The water, as you see, is yellow-hued, wai-lena-lena, a place between mountain and sea where one is free to choose a path in any direction. Here you are welcome to stay."

Ka-nē-loa smiled. The woman was lovely to look at, bathed by the yellow rain and surrounded by the color of the sun. Yet, he reflected, the water seemed yellow because of stirred-up mud and discarded ʻōlena dye, which makes the water unfit for drinking. The healthy glow of her skin could mask the tell-tale signs of jaundice, which yellows the skin as its victim dies.

He spoke to the woman of Lani-huli of these things. "Besides," he said, "if I lived here where the water is yellow, wai-lenalena, I would also be drawn to Wai-lenalena, that valley far up beside Waiʻaleʻale. Truly to stay here is to always be undecided, to go or to stay, to be here or to be there, to start out but return without completing a journey. I shall not remain here."

The woman laughed. "And so you choose to continue," she said. "If and when you find a place to stay, and the woman of your dreams, give her this for me." She tossed the tapa to Ka-nē-loa. As he caught it, the yellow-tinted rain belted down so hard the stream was lost to his view. Then it stopped, the sun shone, and Ka-nē-loa could see no trace of the woman at Lani-huli.

For a moment, he felt a sense of regret at her going. Then he heard, drifting down the stream as if the water itself was singing, the echo of a voice:

> She is gone, the woman of
> Lani-huli.
> 'Ōlena-hued the tapa,
> Beside wai-lenalena.
> Nothing more do you need there.
> Ka-nē-loa, search for me!
> Look beside the singing stream
> Of Waioli!

As he walked farther upstream, the ridges on his right and on his left soared upwards eagerly to their meeting with the mountains. He was climbing a bit now, the great fertile plain now behind and below him. The water of Waioli flowed faster here, murmuring to the moss-covered boulders in its path.

The sun was strong overhead when he came to a grove of forty foot tall trees of 'ōhi'a-'ai, the mountain apple. Growing along each branch, half hidden by dark green leaves, were red-skinned fruit. A living fence of dark green sugar cane surrounded this grove. There was a smell of sweetness in the air, of sugar and 'ōhi'a fruit, that was almost overpowering. The green of the 'ōhi'a leaves, the grass, and the cane darkened and lightened as the wind shifted them. Ka-nē-loa was reminded of the green sea sparkling in the sun, whose every shade of color tells the water's depth, the darker the deeper.

Such a place, Ka-nē-loa had come to realize, housed a woman, perhaps even the one for whom he searched. He waited but no one greeted him. There was only silence, for the small, green birds were too busy gorging on the crisp fruit to sing and even the wind seemed too busy at other things to make a sound. He was tired. He knelt beside the stream, drank deeply, and sat back against the trunk of a tree. His eyes closed.

A woman laughed. Ka-nē-loa's eyes flew wide open. Across the stream sat a woman dressed in green. Her tapa was green, and so was the sheet of coarse, heavy tapa that lay across the beating anvil beside her. Around her head she wore a braided wreath of lacy palapalai fern. There was a pile of 'ōhi'a-'ai fruit before her and she took them up one by one, cut them in half, threw the large seeds to one side, and skewered the slices on coconut rib needles. On her right was a gourd filled with wizened sun-dried fruit. In no other way could this fruit be preserved beyond its season. Now this was a time of intensive work. Later there would be time for other things.

"You sleep," the woman in green chided. "Fine searcher you are. As you see I am too busy to look out for you. It is a good thing I finished this piece of tapa before the fruit was ripe."

As she talked, her fingers and hands flew along the path of their duties, like the hands of a hula dancer.

"Here at Kū-pā-kō-'ili, the standing fence of sugar cane, is the famous grove of 'ōhi'a-'ai trees. Long, long ago these trees were planted by little people whose language sounds like the chittering of birds. Where they live now I do not know, but I come here when the fruit is ripe. I pick the fruit by moonlight and dry them in the sun. Truly this is a good place for you to come."

Ka-nē-loa sighed. This woman in green tapa and palapalai fern was lovely to look at. Her motions were a delight to watch. Yet he felt that if he stayed he would not have time to watch her for he too would become as busy. When the fruit was all dried, what other chores would there be to do? It would not be an unpleasant life, he thought, to be here with this kupa, this native of the place, and to koili, to rest in this place as a bird rests on a branch.

So he thought for quite some time before he replied. "I am sorry," he said, "but I shall not stay. The fruit of the 'ōhi'a-'ai is a laxative. One can only eat a little at a time and never dare to satisfy one's hunger with them. And although you are a native of this place, the kupa, I would rest here, koili like the moon rests upon the sea. I do not need the moon's shadow when it is the sun I seek. This place, Kū-pā-kō-'ili, is not for me."

"Wisely chosen," the woman replied. "I have no time to waste. Take this tapa and some strings of dried 'ōhi'a-'ai fruit. They are yours." The shadows deepened around her and she blended into the green darkness. Only the pale fruit lying on the tapa was left on the other side of the stream.

Sighing through the trees came the echo of a song:

> Wisely chosen indeed at
> Kū-pā-kō-'ili.
> Take the mamaki tapa
> Strong when dry, tearing when wet.
> Nothing more do you need there.
> Ka-nē-loa, search for me!
> Look beside the singing stream
> Of Waioli!

Ka-nē-loa waded the stream and picked up the gifts of the woman in green. Packing them away, he continued to walk along the chattering stream.

Soon he reached a ground of 'ōhi'a lehua trees. It was unexpectedly cold in the shade of these trees, more like Kōke'e on a winter's morning than like the upper valley of Hanalei. The trees were not in bloom, yet a flock of tiny birds flitted among the blue-green leaves. Their pale yellow and green bodies seemed like fluttering leaves newly unfurled and they poked their blue bills here and there, snatching caterpillars and spiders to eat on the wind. They flitted quickly, hardly resting long enough to be seen. They were mountain birds, he knew, living in the swamp far above. What were they doing here?

Beneath the trees was a carpet of 'uki'uki, a lily with long slender leaves, whose light blue berries gleamed in the filtered rays of sunlight. Here and there grew shrubs with large leaves that were covered with a fuzz on the underside.

Dark blue flowers and berries covered the shrubs. It was a beautiful place but the wind was cold and Ka-nē-loa did not wish to stay.

As he walked on, a woman stepped in front of him on the path. Her movements were quick and spritely, her eyes and hands darting about like nimble birds alert to satisfy their curiosity.

"You move on without a rest," she said. Above her, the blue-billed birds flitted from branch to branch and she herself seemed ready to take wing and join them. "But take with you my present. Here is a piece of tapa stained by the pale blue berries of the 'uki-'uki. Remember the lady of the blue-billed birds," she said and, like the little manu'a-kepa above her, winged away among the trees.

Amazed, Ka-nē-loa stood rooted to the spot. This was a strange place, this spot that belonged to the mountains of Kōke'e and not to the banks of the singing waters, Waioli. As he prepared to move on, the voice that was luring him along this strange journey came echoing on the chilly wind:

> Ka-nē-loa, come away
> From Manu'a-kepa.
> Pale blue tapa is
> The gift of the bird woman.
> Nothing more do you need there.
> Ka-nē-loa, search for me,
> Look beside the singing stream
> Of Waioli!

It was mid-afternoon and the shadows were almost as long as the objects that cast them were tall. As Ka-nē-loa climbed higher along the banks of the chattering stream, the groves of trees fell away and the air grew warmer. The hills closed in more and the mountains loomed closer and higher. As he rounded the corner of a hill, a strong scent perfumed the air around him, reminding him of sea salt at Mono-lau, the spicy smell of 'alani, the over sweetness of Kū-pā-kō-'ili. There was also a strong new aroma that overpowered all others and drew him forward to find its source.

Alone in a grassy place beside the stream stood a pū hala tree. The tree was wide-branched, each branch crowned by a twisting bundle of long, saw-toothed leaves. Straight, cylindrical aerial roots descended from each branch in such a way that the startled Ka-nē-loa thought the tree itself was walking toward him. The strong scent radiated from the flowers of this pū hala. Ka-nē-loa was very pleased to see a woman sitting among the aerial roots, and he sat down to speak to her and, he hoped, to stay.

"You have been long on your journey," the woman said.

"It has been long in impressions, if not in distance," he replied, not sure if she were stating a fact or implying a criticism. The loveliness of youth had faded in her, yet now she was a handsome woman, her gleaming eyes holding his attention with their deep color.

"This place, Ka-hala-māpuana, is not far from the beach. I have already been to the seashore and back today," she said. "When the hala is blooming, as it is now, I know the sea urchins are nice and fat. Then I go to the reef and gather some. I have crushed some of the sea urchins and have soaked a piece of tapa in it. Now, you are just in time to help me."

From a bowl she drew out a piece of tapa that had taken on the purple color of the sea urchin's shell. Together they rinsed it in the stream and the water turned the midnight blue of the night sky. They spread the tapa cloth out on the grass and anchored it down with stones so it would not blow away in the wind.

Then she brought out a curved long board and a stone poi pounder. Ka-nē-loa seated himself at one end of this board and began to pound dark purple taro corms into a paste, carefully adding water until the smooth consistency of the paste was just right for eating with two fingers.

The woman, perhaps because of having already done so much, was content to sit back and watch Ka-nē-loa work. He grew dizzy from the strong smell that formed around them like a mist. She was, he noted, older than he had thought at first, a handsome woman, but one who seemed content to let the young man work as she watched. When the hala is blooming, the sea urchins are fat, she had said. That was a fact, indeed. But the hala, in order to bloom, must be quite old, and the sea urchins to be useful for dye must be quite young. And that implied that older people are dependent on the strength of the young. At this time of their lives, their age difference would not matter, but it would in years to come.

Ka-nē-loa struggled to his feet. He wanted to stay, for the rich perfume clouded his mind, promising endless delights. But he knew that when he found the one he was looking for, she would not need such perfume to hold him. "My journey is not yet over," he said. "I must go."

"Stay a while more," the woman said, and the perfume grew stronger and thicker.

"No," he gasped and walked away, stifled and unable to breathe in this atmosphere.

"Wait!" she called. She folded up the dark blue tapa and handed it to him. She smiled at him sadly and the perfume grew so strong, Ka-nē-loa staggered with dizziness. When his senses cleared, nothing remained in the clearing but the pū hala tree, looking as though it were about to stride off down the path on its spider's legs.

A fresh gust of wind blew away the remaining clouds of heavy perfume. The voice carried by the wind seemed stronger, less an echo than the sounds of someone talking just around the corner of the path.

> Heavy are the scents
> Of Ka-hala-māpuana.
> Sea urchin purple tapa
> Is scented with pū hala.
> Nothing more do you need there.
> Ka-nē-loa, search for me,
> Search beside the singing stream
> Of Waioli!

He climbed farther into the foothills. A bank of puffy clouds formed on the slopes of the ridge and spilled over, searching tendrils of cloud seeking the stream. Here, where the clouds formed a backdrop, Ka-nē-loa saw a sad-faced woman. She was sitting idly, her posture, the drooped shoulders, the position of the legs showing Ka-nē-loa a great fatigue. She had drawn a kihei of tapa around her shoulders for it was cool here. On one side of her there was a rubbish pile of broad leaves stained by their own violet sap. The point where the leaf joined its stem was a pale red-blue translucent color. She had been working with the poni taro whose sap was used as a dye. Indeed, her violet-stained hands showed she had been busy. She had made a head wreath of fern and wild violets, the kalili that hides in the mountains. It was obvious she was waiting and struggling to stay awake.

She spoke as he came near. Her voice was low but soothing. "I have been waiting for you, Ka-nē-loa," she said.

"Many women have been waiting for me, it seems," he replied. "I am getting tired."

"Sit down beside me," she offered. "Here, where the clouds mass at the horizon, covering the afternoon sun, here at Ka-uka-'opua, we will rest together and sleep. I am very tired." She yawned and, as often happens, he yawned too, a jaw-splitting yawn that shook his whole body. His eyelids felt heavy, too heavy to keep open.

"Sleep," she murmured, "rest. There is no need to go farther."

He wanted to rest. Sleep soothed his muscles and he almost fell. The singing stream chattered angrily.

"No!" he cried out, heeding the stream's message. "I must go on. To sleep now is wrong."

He stumbled to the stream's edge and splashed cold water over his face and the back of his neck. Sleep fled from the icy touch. He turned and saw no one. Only at the edge of the clouds was a neatly folded tapa. He lifted the violet-colored cloth to his nose and smelled the perfume of kalili, the hidden violet that gave the color its name.

From the cloud bank, the voice he had been following all day called to him:

> Kalili sleeps in the clouds
> Of Ka-uka-'opua.
> Take the violet-scented cloth
> She has made for you, her gift.
> Nothing more do you need there.

Ka-nē-loa, come to me.
Search beside the singing stream
Of Waioli!

Ka-nē-loa plunged into the clouds. Immediately the light grew dim. The clouds swirled thicker and thicker about him, touching him with cold fingers that left beads of dew on his skin. The fog swirled and trees loomed menacing from the darkness, then disappeared again. He shouted, hoping his voice would cause the clouds to disperse, but it was of no help. He stopped, confused. He could not see the path anymore. The solid world had become dim and ghostly, changing shape at will, as though luring the visitor from his path to his doom. All color had faded. Everything was like the clouds themselves, pale gray here, dark gray there.

He stopped and listened. No birds sang. The trees whispered. Even the stream seemed to have fallen silent under the weight of the clouds. Then faintly he heard a whistle. He whistled sharply and loudly to answer it. Whoever it was ahead of him began to whistle a strange tune, almost as though these tinkling sounds were telling secrets, good secrets, secrets better kept untold, secrets of the gods, secrets of parents choosing death in times of famine so their children may eat, secrets between friends, any secret at all!

He followed the sound to the edge of the stream. There on a huge, gray boulder surrounded by rushing water, he saw the figure of a woman, but the clouds shifted so that he could not see her at all clearly. Only the whistling continued, a murmuring soft tune. Then the tune carried words.

"You are at Wai-'ama'o, where even the tinkling water tells secrets. Come and join me where the river runs gray in its bed. I know your secret. Shall I tell it to you?"

"No," he replied. "Everything here is gray and confusing and damp. I shall keep going. Even you, what little I can see, are pale and gray like the face of a sick person. I do not care about your secrets."

"Then take this with you," the gray woman said. "Here is a choice tapa, he pele, dyed with the charcoal of burned sugar cane that has been mixed with coconut milk and scented with maile."

The clouds swirled around her. Ka-nē-loa picked his way carefully from rock to rock until he reached the tapa. There was no sign of the pale woman. Only the echo of whistling like far off birds could be heard. Riding over these faint sounds was the voice:

> Pale and gray, my sister's face
> At Wai-'ama'o.
> What is the whistled secret?
> Why the gray pele tapa?
> Bring it, join them together!
> Ka-nē-loa, do you search?
> Find me where the singing stream
> Of Waioli begins!

Ka-nē-loa was tired. For a moment he thought of returning to his canoe and setting sail again. But, as he looked about him, he realized that the waterfall he had seen as a thin line of water far away was now thundering in a mighty torrent of water almost on his head. He could almost touch the steep cliff down which the great waterfall, Nā-molokama, flowed. There was not much stream left to search. Having come this far, he decided, he might as well continue on.

The clouds swirled around him, blocking his view. The walls of fern-covered rocks were steep and the stream squeezed past them, pushing impatiently against the huge boulders blocking its way. The rocks were slippery with moss. Ka-nē-loa stepped from one to another gingerly, for there was no path now, only dark, mossy rocks in the stream itself. Then there were no more rocks. The clouds swirled deeper around him and it grew dark, too dark to see, yet he sensed that there was a deep pool of water in front of him. He sat on the last stone and placed the bundles of tapa beside him and listened.

There was the sound of the babbling stream behind him. The water lapped his feet as it rippled past. There was the sound of rain falling onto water that echoed from wall to wall of a small enclosed space. But there was no song, no voice calling to him.

"I have come," he said quietly. "Have you no greeting for me? Have I missed you? Were you one of those women I passed today? Yet each gave me a gift for you."

As he spoke, he unfolded each tapa and threw it, like a fisherman casting his net, onto the surface of the pond before him.

"These are the gifts," he said.

> The red tapa from Mono-lau;
> The orange tapa from Māhā-mōkū;
> The yellow tapa of Lani-huli;
> The green tapa of Kū-pā-kō-'ili;
> The blue tapa of Manu'a-kepa;
> The indigo tapa of Ka-hala-māpuana;
> The violet tapa from Ka-uka-'opua;
> And the gray tapa of Wai-'ama'o.

These are the gifts I was given and, in turn, give to you!"

The tapa sheets floated on the water, swirled here and there by the ripples until they melded together. The clouds began to dissolve, growing lighter and breaking into a fine mist. The air was filled with mist drifting here and there like lazy schools of fish. Now Ka-nē-loa saw that he sat on the edge of a great pool of water surrounded by fern-covered walls of shiny black wet rock. Into this pool fell the great waterfall of Nā-molokama as a gentle rain. It was dark here, no color save the gray of the clouds.

The tapa sheets dissolved as the clouds disappeared and the late afternoon sun shone brilliantly into the mist. Each droplet of water reflected all the colors of the tapa sheets floating in the water, their colors shifting as the wind played with them. The multicolored mist gathered over the place where the tapa sheets floated. Through a curtain of shifting colored light, Ka-nē-loa became aware that a woman was in the pond. Around her was an arc of seven colors, gleaming layers pulsing and deepening in tone and density until the arc was no longer made of light but were solid panels of pure color.

"Ānuenue!" he whispered. Fear and wonder filled him, for this was the sister of the great gods, Kāne and Kanaloa.

She held out her hands to him, welcoming him as she walked toward him. At last he heard her voice issuing from her own throat, no longer an echo on the wind.

> Ka–nē–loa,
> Ānuenue greets you!
> Only you have found the way
> To bring Kauai the rainbow.
> Come to me, Ka–nē–loa.
> Hidden was I beside the singing water
> Of Waioli.
> Ka–nē–loa,
> Ānuenue greets you!

HŌLUA-MANU

CHRISTINE FAVÉ 1982

HŌLUA-MANU

Soon after the Hawaiian people settled Kauai, a man and woman climbed up a canyon and followed a stream that came to be known as Waimaka. Where Ōpae-wela valley joins 'Ōma'o valley the couple made their home. Fresh water flowed near their doorstep, taro grew wild, and fresh-water shrimp, the 'ōpae, were easy to catch and delicious to eat. Best of all, they had a young son who was full of energy and flew from place to place, earning him the name of Manu, bird.

Manu's parents became lazy. They sat on lauhala mats spread out under a milo tree and watched Manu fly from place to place finding, preparing, cooking, and serving the food they ate. Their bodies grew fatter and they moved less and less, but their eyes darted swiftly, searching for the moment to amuse themselves.

This couple had two strange abilities. They were able to lift rocks into the air, move them about, and put them down in a new place. These two lazy ones enjoyed dropping rocks near unwary strangers that came along the trail from 'Ōmao valley. The stranger, besieged with rocks mysteriously falling on him from the sky above, leaped, cavorted, and cowered, giving the malicious jokesters great pleasure. They could also send freshets of water rushing down the stream bed at will. Whenever strangers would try to cross the stream, a flash flood would tumble them off their feet, drenching them from head to foot. Seeing this, the jokesters would laugh until their laughter would echo from the valley walls.

Soon strangers did not come very often into Waimaka, so the lazy parents sought their amusement by lifting stones and dropping them as close to their son as possible to see him jump with surprise and sudden fear. Whenever Manu had to cross the stream, his parents sent down a freshet to try to knock him off his feet, and whenever it did, the shouts of his parents' laughter echoed in the hills. Whenever it was time to eat, however, the lazy parents shouted for Manu to bring the calabash of poi and fresh 'ōpae to them, and whatever else he had managed to find for them to eat, from wild bananas to hō'i'o fern.

"What use is a strong son," Manu's father complained whenever the food was slow in coming, "if he will not work for his parents?"

So Manu worked hard from morning to night. Even then, before he was allowed to sleep, he had to prepare strings of kukui nuts and set them ablaze so that his parents could see while they drank the fermented 'awa made from roots of the plants Manu found far away in Wai'ale'ale. Their drunken shouts disturbed his sleep, although the sound of rocks falling outside the little cave where he slept no longer bothered him.

Almost every family, in those far off days, had its own taro patch. Manu's parents, of course, had never made one, his father being too lazy to dig the patch or to cultivate it. Manu, then, had to search the valleys for wild taro. He learned where the 'ahē-ke'oke'o, the wild white taro, grew and he learned where the 'ahē-'ula'ula, the red taro, grew. But such wild taro, left to itself, was not ready for eating all year round and Manu learned to plant it, a little each day, so that there would be taro ready for eating throughout the year. On the upland slopes and forest clearings he would dig a hole and fill it with rotting leaves and plant his taro. Along the bank of streams he would heap up piles of mud and plant his taro there.

This meant that he spent most of his days walking far distances. The farther he went, the longer he was away from his parents. The longer he was away, the more time they had to send rocks and freshets to cause him trouble. He grew very agile learning to dodge rocks and hurry over a streambed before the freshet could reach him. What time he had when not searching for food he had to spend in preparing it. It was Manu who had to dig the imu, steam the taro, peel it, pound it and form it into small cakes to dry in the sun. These cakes would keep for a long time and Manu hoped that one day he would have enough of these to give him some time off.

Manu had a dream.

When he went down the stream to catch shrimp and gather wi, the freshwater limpets, he came near a hōlua slide. The hōlua slide was a specially built platform, high at one side on a hillside, low and flat on the other. Down this steep slope, chiefly men and women would throw themselves onto long, narrow sleds and speed down the slide like lightning. It was a dangerous pasttime. The sled was very narrow and the slightest bump on the slope could send it over the side to break itself and its rider on the rocks. Manu could think of nothing he would rather do than ride a sled down the hōlua slide. There was never time to make a sled for himself, however, or to slide down the slide even if he had a sled, for there were always too many things he had to do to feed his parents. Only at night, when his soul was free while his body slept, could Manu dream of flying down the hōlua.

One evening, as the yellow clouds edged the eastern ridges, Manu, returning home with a bundle of taro strapped to his back, stumbled across a new hōlua slide. As he stood looking at it in amazement, a tiny sled, a papa hōlua, came hurtling down the slope. It hit a pebble and sped out into the air, tipping off the rider. Manu ran forward and caught the rider in mid-air, saving him from death on the rocks.

Manu set the little hōlua rider down, gazing at him with frank curiosity. The rider was hardly half as tall as Manu, a very small man with a curly brown beard. Manu was about to speak, but the little man darted off into the bushes so quickly that Manu was not sure where he had hidden. Manu smiled sadly for he would have liked to have someone to talk to about hōlua sliding.

He picked up his load of taro and started homeward. He saw the tiny sled where it lay broken on some rocks. He picked it up and looked it over, running his fingers along the long slender runners. "Too bad it's broken," he murmured. "But maybe I can fix it." And in fixing it, he thought, he could learn how to make one for himself. He strapped the sled to his back and trudged home.

"Where have you been, lazy boy?" his parents scolded when he reached home. "We are waiting for our supper and already it is almost dark. The kukui nuts are not yet strung together either." Manu hurried to prepare the evening meal and to string together the kukui nuts. Tonight he desperately wanted time for himself while there was still light enough to see.

"Cold food!" Manu's parents were astonished as Manu set before them a calabash of yesterday's poi and a handful each of 'ōpae and wi. While they ate and later drank their 'awa in the light of burning kukui nuts, Manu sat out of their sight but where the light, too, helped him. He took up the papa hōlua he had brought home with him. It was small and very well made. Two of the crosspieces had been broken by the fall. He ran his fingers lovingly over the pieces, learning how they fit together, planning how to make a sled big enough for himself.

In the days that followed, Manu found wood and shaped it to replace the broken crosspieces. When the sled was mended, he polished it with kukui oil until it gleamed in the light and its runners shone smooth.

But Manu's parents were not happy. "If you have time to make a papa hōlua," they muttered, "it shows what a lazy boy you are. Thinking only of your own pleasure, not of honoring your parents. How can you do this to us?"

"I have never ridden a papa hōlua," Manu answered. "I work from morning to evening to find food for us all. If only once I could have a day to myself, I would do nothing but slide down the hōlua."

"Then take a day off from work," answered his parents. Manu was surprised by this sudden generosity. However, his pleasure did not last long, for his parents continued. "First you must fill a large imu with food for us. And why don't you build a loʻi, a taro patch with fresh water flowing through it, nearby so we can get taro if we want it. You must also plant some sugar cane and some bananas, too. If you do all this in the next three days, you may have one day all for yourself."

"You are unkind to tease me," protested Manu. "You know I can't do all those things in three days."

"Don't say we are unkind," his parents said, enjoying their latest joke. "We are willing to let you play, providing you do the work first."

The next time Manu went up to the place where he had caught the hōlua rider, he took the little sled with him. He found the paved slide without trouble and placed the repaired papa hōlua at the top where it would be found. Then he went farther up the valley searching for wild taro.

As he came down the trail in the late afternoon, the little bearded man appeared suddenly in the path in front of Manu. He was holding the repaired sled.

"I have come to thank you," the little man said.

"I have done nothing," answered Manu.

"You saved me from the rocks when I fell from my papa hōlua," the little man pointed out. "And you repaired my sled. Truly, you have done much."

Manu was embarrassed about being thanked. No one had ever thanked him before and he did not know how to answer. "I would do as much for anyone," he stammered.

"But you did it for me," said the little man. "That is what is important. And so, I thank you, my friend."

"No one has ever thanked me before," said Manu in slow appreciation.

The little man replied, "I have prepared a meal for us, a small token of my thanks." He sat on the ground and opened a ti-wrapped bundle of food. There were steamed taro, fish and taro leaves, ʻōpae, and the fiddleheads of hōʻiʻo. These were foods that Manu himself found and prepared, but no one, for as long as he could remember, had ever prepared food for him. He put down his bundle of wild taro and sat beside the little man and ate with him.

After they were through eating, the little man asked, "Why do you spend all your time, day after day, searching for wild foods in the valleys and mountains? Why don't you go sledding once in a while? I have seen you watching the hōlua riders with longing."

"I would like nothing more," Manu replied simply. "But first I must make a taro patch near the river so that I don't have to go so far to find taro. I must also plant sugar cane and wauke. Then perhaps I will have a little free time to myself."

"Come sledding with me now," urged the little man. "There is a slide nearby, as you know, and my sled awaits you."

"I cannot," Manu said sadly. "Your slide is too short for me, and your sled would not carry my weight. I am late already and my parents will be angry enough. I haven't prepared anything for their meal tonight." He sighed deeply as he picked up his bundle and strapped it to his back.

"But one day," he said, "I will do what I would like to do. One day I will have put aside enough food for my parents and I will go sledding from sunrise to sunset."

With that, Manu thanked the little man and walked slowly homeward. As he had expected, his parents were angry with him and sent him out again to find more ʻōpae for them, since they had eaten all he had caught the day before. As he turned over the stones in the stream, his nimble fingers searching out the hidden shrimp, his parents sent down a freshet which tumbled Manu in its rapids. The shouts of his parents' delighted laughter echoed from the hills. But this time, unknown to Manu or his parents, other ears heard the echoing laughter and were not amused.

During the night, while Manu slept, the hum of a thousand tiny voices filled the air and all during that night the murmur of voices surrounded Manu's home. As dawn came, the sound faded into the ridges and mountain reaches.

When Manu's parents awoke, they looked about them with astonishment. Beside their house was a taro patch surrounded by solid stone walls so intricately fitted together that water did not leak through. A ditch brought water from the stream above into the loʻi and young taro plants nodded in the morning breeze, their feet firmly pressed into the mud with the cool water flowing over them. Sugar cane had been planted along the walls. Banana plants stood in profusion where water from the 'auwai could be let out upon them, for bananas like the damp. There were also many calabashes set on the lau hala mat filled with food still warm from the imu.

Manu smiled. "Now I can go hōlua sliding," he said.

"No, no," his parents said, "there is no wi here. You must go get some wi from the stream."

But Manu refused. "The things you said I must do have been done. I must go up the valley to thank those who did these things for us in one night. Then I am going to go down to the hōlua slide. Perhaps someone will loan me a papa hōlua so that I may slide at least once."

"Ungrateful boy," his parents scolded. "You refuse to do such a little thing for us after all we have done for you?"

"What have you done for me?" Manu asked.

"What have we done?" his parents cried in astonishment.

"I carried you within me and gave birth to you!" his mother exclaimed. "And the pain you caused me!"

"I fed you and clothed you and guided your first footsteps. I cared for you when you were ill. Ungrateful boy!" his father scolded.

"Stay home! Do your work!" they demanded in unison.

But Manu turned away from them. He had worked hard for many years. They had promised him a day to himself if certain tasks were done, and by some miracle those tasks were done. He was free. He went up the valley to the little hōlua slide to search for his friend, the brown-bearded man.

"Where are you?" he called. "Come out so that I can thank you."

"No thanks necessary," the little man said as he stepped out into the open. "You saved my life. But the best is still to come."

The little man led Manu to the top of the ridge. From here Manu could look down on the right into Loli valley. On the left flowed the 'Ōpaewela stream. "Look down," the little man said. "What do you see?"

"A hōlua slide!" Manu said in amazement. "A wonderful hōlua slide!"

A long course had been made of rocks fitted together so well that they formed a smooth path for the headlong rush of the sled. Over this stone facing, grass had been laid to make the slope slippery and very fast. The slide extended down the slope of the ridge and the end seemed to stretch right into the stream sparkling far below them.

At Manu's look of surprise, the little man laughed. "Yes, we made this last night. I am a Menehune chief. Does that surprise you? No matter. Come, let us race."

Manu's face fell in sorrow. "I have no sled," he said.

"Would we build you a slide and provide no papa hōlua for it?" the Menehune chief laughed. He whistled twice and a group of Menehune came bearing two sleds, one the size of the chief, one taller than Manu himself.

The chief pointed to the long papa hōlua. "Take it," he said. "It's yours."

Manu took the papa hōlua gently in his hands. The sled was six yards long. The two runners were of māmane wood, tapered so that the sled rested on a thin knife's edge. Nine inches wide, it was lashed strongly together. Across the top was a narrow platform of koa wood over which was a matting of finely woven lauhala. The papa hōlua had been rubbed with kukui oil until it shone brilliantly in the sunshine.

"Let us race!" the Menehune chief shouted. Grabbing his papa hōlua, he ran for the slide, threw himself onto the sled, and sped down the slope. Manu followed him and at long last found himself flying downhill with the ease of a bird and the speed of the wind.

His parents, sitting angrily under their tree, watched Manu. The sound of his laughter echoed from the valley walls. "I have never heard him laugh before," his father muttered. "I don't like the sound."

"We must do something to stop it quickly," his mother said. "Otherwise he will never work for us again but will stay on the hōlua, sledding all day long."

They concentrated their powers and, as the two men climbed to the top of the ridge again, two great rocks rose in the air and settled down in the middle of the hōlua.

Reaching the top again, Manu flung himself onto the slide. He immediately saw the huge rocks his parents had placed there and with great skill he jumped high, lifting the papa hōlua with him, skimming over the rocks and landing unhurt on the other side.

His parents were even angrier to see how he had avoided their obstacles.

"Come and work, lazy boy!" they yelled.

Manu looked across the stream at them and replied, "I have worked for you without complaining, doing all that you asked of me. Now it is time for me to enjoy myself for a little while."

On his way back to the top of the slide, Manu kicked one of the huge rocks into the Waimaka stream where the rock remains today. Once at the top, for the third time Manu and the Menehune chief flew down the hōlua.

His angry parents sent a flood down the stream. The freshet and Manu met at the bottom of the slide and Manu was tumbled about in the fierce water and his sled was smashed. The sound of his parents' laughter echoed in the valley.

Manu picked up his broken papa hōlua. There would be no more hōlua sliding that day.

"Come now," his parents called. "Work for us. You will never beat the floods we will send against you."

Manu came to where they sat. Quietly he said to them, "For twenty years I have worked hard for you. I have worked day and night, always doing what you have asked, and over the years you have asked more and more of me as you yourselves did less and less. You have wasted the gifts the gods gave you, your power over rocks and water. Look at the taro lo'i the Menehune made. You could have made that yourselves with very little effort. You could even have made the hōlua slide, for it is, after all, only made of rocks. This whole valley could have been turned into taro patches and kept properly irrigated at all times and there would have been plenty of food right at hand. Instead, because you toss rocks and send freshets against visitors for your selfish amusement, no one comes and this valley is deserted and overgrown. If the gods saw this, they would take your gifts away.

"And you have broken your promise to me. You promised me a day of hōlua sliding in return for completing three tasks you set for me. The tasks were done, and yet you refuse to let me enjoy this one day. I know now you will never be satisfied. Lead your own lives. I shall live mine."

He picked up his sled and without glancing back climbed the ridge. His parents called to him to return but he didn't listen to them. They directed their powers to send a freshet of raging water to block his path, but this time the torrent did not come. Manu's parents ordered rocks to fly down in front of him and drive him back to them but no rock moved. The gods had taken back their gifts and this couple was now forced to work for themselves to earn their food.

Manu repaired his sled and day after day he raced with the Menehune chief. His skill grew until he could ride the papa hōlua standing up, guiding the slender sled by shifting the weight of his body. Manu's fame as a hōlua racer spread over the island and chiefs came to compete with him. From every corner of the island, people came to Hōlua-manu to watch Manu race and cheer his skill and daring.

UA

CHRISTINE FAYÉ '83

UA

Long before Kauai was ruled by one chief, there were two villages in the Waimea district. One was by the shore where the river enters the sea. The other was far up the canyon where the Koaiʻe stream joins the Waimea. The shore people fished and wove lau hala mats and baskets. The upland people made olonā ropes and made spears, paddles, and tapa-beaters from the hard wood of the Koaiʻe. The two villages traded the things they made but in no other way did they come to know one another. Each village kept closely to itself.

Because suspicion grows in ignorance, there came a time when each village thought the other was cheating, so the two went to war. When the war was over, neither side had won and were farther apart than before. The trading stopped. No longer did the Waimea folk have rope and paddles. No longer did the Koaiʻe people have fish and mats. And a man who lived between the two villages where the Waiʻalae stream enters the Waimea decided it would be safer to move to Nuʻalolo until the war was forgotten.

So the man and his wife wrapped their infant daughter in soft tapa to keep her warm and to muffle any noise she might make. They climbed the steep trail to Kukui hill and traveled across Kōkeʻe. Two days later they reached the swinging rope ladder of Nuʻalolo. This ladder was the only way in and out of the valley and it swayed and twisted out over the ocean and the black rocks below.

The man balanced on the ladder and reached for the child. He grasped the tapa and, as he swung the child to him, the tapa ripped. In silent agony, the parents watched their child falling down the cliff to the ocean below, as a gentle rain misted about them as though the clouds themselves grieved.

This was the period of time, however, when the gods had not grown disgusted with mankind and still walked the earth. And so it was that the goddess Ānuenue appeared beneath the falling child in the shape of a rainbow, its colors blazing through the gentle rain. The child fell onto the rainbow which circled around her like protective arms. The sorrowing parents watched the rainbow and their daughter fade, leaving them to wonder at their child's fate.

The rainbow goddess took the infant child into the Koaiʻe canyon to a cave beneath a waterfall fed by the waters of Kōkeʻe. There the infant lived and grew, watched over by the goddess who always appeared as a rainbow. The mists of the falls shone in colors reflected from the small rainbow that hovered over the child's head. The goddess taught her how to invoke the rains that fed the stream, the gentle misting rain, the fine wind-blown rain, the drenching rain, the heavy rain. She also learned to weave hats of 'alae and floated them down the stream where Koai'e women found them and wore them proudly as marks of special favor from the mysterious young woman who lived upstream. Soon she was known as the Rainbow Princess for no one knew of any other name for her.

The people of Koai'e came to the rainbow princess asking her help for rains to feed the upland farmland. The farmers brought her offerings of food, steamed taro, baked sweet potatoes, and handfuls of 'ōpae plucked from the streams. The paddle-makers asked for heavy rains to flood the river below in order to annoy the Waimea folk living on the shore. The Koai'e folk thought of the rainbow princess as their natural leader and soon no decisions were made without first consulting her wisdom. Her answer to their requests could be read in the rain and the clouds which formed around the pool and canyon where she lived, and no one could recall hearing her voice.

Tales of this strange woman and of her great beauty traveled over the island. Visitors, coming with offerings to the rainbow-hued waterfall, peeked shyly at the princess as she sat on the rocks outside her cave. The visitors exclaimed in wonder at the circular rainbow that floated above her head, and they went away again to spread the tale of the wonders they had seen. Those who had smiled in pleasure walked home in misting rains proudly wearing 'alae hats sold them by the Koai'e folk. Those who had been rude and stared and pointed stumbled home in heavy downpours that tore at their hats and unravelled them.

Eventually the tales of this strange rainbow woman reached the ears of the rulers of Waimea village. The chiefess listened and turned to her mother, Kāmū. "What do you make of this tale?" she asked, for she knew that age gives experience and experience leads to wisdom.

Kāmū smiled and gently shrugged her shoulders. She knew her answer would not be heard and indeed the chiefess was already murmuring, "Perhaps she will make a suitable wife for our son."

The chief shook his head in sorrow. He was giving up his hopes of becoming a grandfather. "I doubt it," he said. "No woman has captured his attention, much less his love."

And this was true. The young man, Kulu-'i-ua, was tall and strong. His dark eyes would fill women's thoughts with hopes and dreams, but he did not answer their yearning looks. Again and again the chief and chiefess would bring forward a woman, hoping their son would consent to make her his wife. When he refused, the chief would glare at Kāmū. When Kulu-'i-ua had been born, his grandmother Kāmū had made his parents promise never to force the youngster to marry. She offered no reason for demanding this and many a time the chief regretted giving his promise.

"We can't do anything with him," the chief grumbled. "He will die without being married. I shall never have a grandchild to care for me in my old age." Kulu-'i-ua was the only child and in him lay all his father's thwarted dreams.

"Let's send him to see this rainbow princess," replied the chiefess. "It can't do any harm. It will give him a change of air, at least. But he will not go if I ask him," continued the shrewd chiefess. She turned to her mother. "You must tell him to go."

Kāmū smiled gently and nodded her head in agreement. She went to find her grandson and sat beside him silently. She drew a rainbow in the sand and pointed upriver into the canyon.

"Why should I go?" Kulu-'i-ua demanded, quick to guess his grandmother's meaning. "I have seen many beautiful women. This is a woman like all the others."

"How many women are surrounded by the rainbow?" Kāmū asked.

"I see I must go," the young man responded. "There will be no peace for me until I do."

Of course a young chief from Waimea would not be permitted to travel up-river into the Koai'e territory with his retinue of men and women. The war was not forgotten. So he went alone, stepping from the path when voices warned him of other travelers.

Late one afternoon, he pushed aside the branches of a koai'e and found himself on the edge of the pond into which the waterfall fell. On a rock on the other side of the pool, poised like a startled bird, stood the maiden of the rainbow. Her dark hair flowed down her back like Hanalei's Nā-molokama as it falls from the mountain top to the valley floor. Her skin, glistening with fine mist, shone with the rainbow's seven colors.

Kulu-'i-ua stood as a man suddenly pierced by a spear. He could not look away and he knew in that moment why no other woman had moved him. He murmured, "I have never seen beauty such as yours." The indifference of his heart melted away. "You are the woman I will live for! Come with me and be my wife!"

Her laughter rang about him, echoing from the canyon walls. Kulu-'i-ua was not offended by her laughter for it was not cruel. He was warmed by it, as he was by the soft, misty rain that swept down the canyon and over him.

The rainbow maiden called, "When you can call me by name, I will come to you." Then she stepped behind the waterfall and seemed to melt away like the rainbow itself.

Kulu-'i-ua went into the Koai'e village. There, he thought, he could learn the name of the lovely rainbow maiden. But no one there was sure of her name. He searched out the oldest inhabitant of the village, hoping that his wisdom would help.

"Perhaps her name is Ānuenue, the rainbow," suggested the old man. "Have you called her that?"

"No," replied the young chief and ran for the waterfall. He burst through the trees and stood across the pool from the young maiden. "Ānuenue!" he called. "Come to me!"

She shook her head sadly. "Call me by my true name," she said. "I can come only to the man who learns my name." Again, she disappeared behind the curtain of water.

Kulu-'i-ua returned to the old man of Koai'e. "Ānuenue is not her name," he said.

The old man thought. He did not know her name, but experience told him that guessing sometimes worked. He said, "What about Wai-lele, the waterfall?"

The young man rushed to the pool. "Wai-lele!" he called. Her laugh mingled with the waterfall's sound, but she did not come.

The old man, when Kulu-'i-ua returned to seek another name, put a bowl of poi beside the young man. "You have not eaten today," the old man said.

"When love is burning you in its fires, there isn't time for eating," the young man answered unhappily and pushed the bowl away.

The old man remembered love's fires and how they burned. "What is so marvellous about this woman?" he asked.

"Have you seen her?" the young chief replied. "She shames the rainbow that floats above her. I must learn her name."

"Perhaps she does not have one," the old man said. He was tired of guessing names and would rather be eating the poi. He took up the bowl and dipped in a finger.

"Surely she has a name," Kulu-'i-ua protested. "But what is it?"

The old man, however, was no longer listening. He was intent upon cleaning the bowl of its poi. Young men thought of love and old men thought of food. Kulu-'i-ua flung himself on a sleeping mat and groaned in agony. Every time a possible name occurred to the young chief or the old man, the young chief rushed to the pool but soon returned beaten down by discouragement. He refused all food and drink for so long that the old man grew alarmed that the young man would die. The old man got some friends to carry the dying visitor down the canyon one night and dump him outside Waimea village. The Waimea folk, reasoned the old man, could arrange the funeral. It would serve them right. Since the war, the old man had not had any succulent ocean fish to eat.

Kulu-'i-ua was found in the morning and carried home to his parents.

His mother hovered over him, ready to soothe and comfort as she had always done. "What is wrong?" she asked anxiously.

"I love her," Kulu-'i-ua whispered. "I will not eat until I learn her name."

"I'll get her name for you," the chiefess promised. She hurried away to order a tempting meal for him, but he would not eat. For once, her promise that all would be well did not bend him to her ways.

The chiefess was horrified. If it hadn't been for her husband and her mother sending her son off to look at this rainbow woman, her son would not be lying here like this, his head turned away from his own mother, facing the wall. The chiefess grew angry. She rushed to her husband. "Do something!" she demanded.

The chief sent for every priest, diviner, riddle-guesser, seer and sorcerer on the island. "Tell me her name," he ordered. All of these seers retired to commune with their gods and seek omens in such ways as they used. But the rock mirrors in the calabashes of water reflected only the rainbow shining in the falling mists of the waterfall. Cloud shapes refused to divulge the secret name, but only rained on the kahuna, sending him indoors. Schools of fish only dove deep out of sight as gentle rains spotted the ocean's surface. One by one the seers returned to say the gods were not willing to tell the rainbow woman's name.

Kulu-'i-ua sighed and despaired. He grew thinner and weaker with each passing day. His mother's anger at her husband grew. She glared at her husband. The chief counted the knobs of bone clearly visible down his son's back.

"There are other islands, other seers," the chief said, and sent his retainers to search out the kahuna of the other islands and ask their help.

One by one, the retainers came back. None had discovered the name of the young woman of the rainbow. At last there were no kahuna left to ask. The strength left Kulu-'i-ua's body and his flesh melted away.

"Eat!" urged his mother with tearful desperation. Kulu-'i-ua turned his head away.

"He's dying," the chiefess wept. She turned on her husband. The chief shrugged his shoulders. He too was grieving. There was nothing more he could think of to do. He sat beside his son and waited, dreading what it was he waited for.

The light from the doorway darkened as Kāmū, mother of the chiefess, entered and asked sarcastically, "What is this nonsense?"

The chief and chiefess glared at her. Kāmū chuckled as she sat down beside her grandson. "What fools you are," she said, meaning all three of them. "At least I came before it is too late. No thanks to you." She glared at her daughter and son-in-law until they bowed their heads in shame, for they had not thought to tell her her grandson was dying.

Kāmū looked at her grandson, at the feverish look in his face, at his thin body. "What's the matter with you?" she asked in a tart voice.

"Grandmother," he whispered. "I die for love of the rainbow woman."

"Go and tell her you love her," Kāmū replied. A patter of rain fell on the house, and Kāmū smiled. "She will listen to you."

"Each time I went to see her," the young man said sadly, "she would shake her head and laugh and disappear from my sight. She tells me that when I can call her by name, she will come to me."

"Well, call her by name, then," Kāmū said tartly. Young people, she knew, tended to overlook the obvious. "What could be simpler than that?"

"I have called her a hundred names. She does not come." He spoke with force and anger. He was not the fool his grandmother's words implied.

Kāmū laughed. His spark of anger was a good sign and it pleased her.

"Don't laugh at my love," protested Kulu-'i-ua.

"Why not?" she chuckled, looking at his affectionately. "I do not doubt your love for her. I am laughing at how difficult you have made things for yourself. All of you!" She stared at the chief and chiefess. It was amazing how stupid people could be over simple things.

The chief, reacting to the criticism, protested. "We have searched everywhere to find the girl's name."

"Everywhere but under your nose," retorted Kāmū.

Sarcastically, the chief snarled, "And I suppose you know her name?"

"Certainly I know her name," Kāmū said. "I know it well."

Kulu-'i-ua looked at her in amazement. Joy flooded his body and he struggled to sit up. "Tell me! Tell me!" he begged. "Let me call her!"

"Not until the flesh returns to your body," Kāmū said firmly. She looked at her grandson and her lips curled with distaste. "Look at you!" Nothing but skin and bones! I would not come to you were you to call me by name a thousand times! Nor will she."

Kāmū gestured to the chiefess. "Fetch food and drink," she ordered. "He will eat." The chiefess leapt to her feet and happily ran to select the finest morsels for her son's pleasure.

The young chief willingly wolfed down his food. He ate, swam, ate again, exercised, and ate more of the food his mother always had at hand. His skin became taut and glowed with health. He laughed and played in the misty rains that swept down from the mountains of Kōke'e. His grandmother watched his progress carefully and one day beckoned him to her side.

"Have you ever heard the proverb, 'It takes the gentle pressure of rain to open the lehua flower'?" Kāmū asked the happy young man. "Well, you are like the lehua bud seeking to reach full bloom. And this girl surrounded by the rainbow? What is the rainbow but sun and rain? And what is your name, Kulu-'i-ua? Go. Call her by name, her true name and yours. It is Ua, the rain."

With the speed of the 'i'iwi bird soaring on the winds, Kulu-'i-ua sped to the pond where his loved one lived. He looked at the rainbow maiden and laughed with pure joy.

"Ua!" he called. "Ua!" And he spread open his arms for her.

A soft rain came and the sun shone and the rainbow blazed in all its colors. Ua smiled. "You have called my true name," she said. "I will come with you."

To celebrate the marriage, the Waimea villagers and the folk of Koai'e met together where the Wai'alae stream enters the Waimea. They were afraid of each other, yet proud. The rainbow maiden was the leader of Koai'e. The young chief would be the leader of Waimea. The people of each village stayed on their side of the river.

Kāmū, the wise one, stood on a high rock and lifted her hand for silence and attention. Below her stood Kulu-'i-ua and Ua. Around them shone the colors of the rainbow and above their heads shimmered the rainbow itself.

"Friends!" Kāmū called. "Be friends indeed! And from now on, be joined as one people, as these two are joined together. Free to share your lau hala mats and 'alae hats, free to share the ocean fish and the koai'e wood. No longer enemies but joined together under Ua and Kulu-'i-ua, the beginning of the time when all Kauai shall come together as one people! Now, celebrate and dance and feast and tell stories!"

Friends, old and new, shouted in gladness and surged together to celebrate. When the festivities were over, they found themselves truly as one people, for Ua and Kulu-'i-ua, favored ones of the rainbow goddess, brought peace and prosperity to their land.

KAWELO O MĀNĀ

KAWELO O MĀNĀ

Early in the morning, when the sun rested on Waiʻaleʻale before leaping into the sky, the fishermen of Mānā arose from their beds. They walked down the trail that led from their village on the edge of the marshes where Limaloa's mirage appears, past the cultivated lands of Kawelo, to the sea.

No matter how early they were, Kawelo was already busy in his ʻuala fields. He would always be there crouching down amongst the heart-shaped leaves of the sweet potato. His kīhei, knotted at his right shoulder, covered him from neck to heel from the cool morning air.

"Good morning, Kawelo!" the fishermen called out as they passed the crouching farmer.

Kawelo's fingers grasped the edge of his kīhei as the early morning sea breeze tugged at it. "Good morning, men of Mānā," Kawelo answered. "The sun shines brightly there on the mountains and the breeze plays gently. It will be a good day."

"A good day, indeed," agreed the fishermen on their way to their canoes on the beach.

"Look to it the bananas are put away!" warned Kawelo.

"Have no fear," laughed the men of Mānā. "Our wives know that!" Their footsteps quickened for fear that Kawelo would tell the errant wind that they planned to fish and the breeze would tell the fish and so warn them.

But Kawelo knew better than to tell Koʻolau-wahine, the sea breeze, the fishermen's plans. He knew that no one must mention to a fisherman anything about going fishing. Nor could the fishermen's wives eat bananas while their husbands were gone. To do any of these things was to bring bad luck to fishermen. And, catching no fish, they would return home early. Kawelo did not want that. He only teased the fishermen to test the seriousness of their purpose.

As the fishermen continued on their way to the shore, one said, "Kawelo is a very pleasantly spoken man."

"Indeed," said another. "And very industrious."

"We never see him except when he is working in his fields," said a third. "He lives alone."

"But he grows the best sweet potatoes, delicious to taste!" They reached the shore and all thought of Kawelo faded as they set about their day's business.

As the sun climbed higher into the sky, the women of Mānā went down to the sea along the path that passed Kawelo's farm. They were going to the groves of hala to weave the leaves into mats and baskets. It was a long, tedious occupation but one that was pleasant enough in company, seated in dappled shade as the sea breeze fanned their faces. "Good morning, Kawelo!" they called gaily to the farmer as he squatted in his ʻuala field.

"The sun climbs well into the sky," Kawelo said. His fingers grasped the edges of his kīhei as the mischievous breeze tugged at it. "It is a good day for weaving mats of lau hala."

"A good day, indeed!" the women of Mānā replied.

"Look to it that the little children do not stray too far away," Kawelo warned.

"Have no fear," they answered. "We will not let the little children out of our sight."

As the women continued along the path to the beach, one said, "He is very pleasantly spoken."

"He always has a cheerful word to say," said another. "And he is a very hard working man."

"He eats well," remarked a third. "He is well fleshed."

The women of Mānā reached the beach and all thought of Kawelo faded as they set about their day's business.

When the sun had reached the top of its climb and rested before starting the long slide to the western sea, the youngsters of Mānā left their village to go to the sea to swim and surf in the waves.

"Good morning, Kawelo!" they called as they passed the farmer, crouching in his ʻuala field.

"Good morning, youngsters," answered Kawelo. "The sun rests in its journey." His fingers caught the edge of his kīhei for the busy breeze was trying to flip it over his back. "It is a beautiful day for swimming and surfing in the waves."

"A wonderful day!" exclaimed the youngsters.

"Look to it as you play," cautioned Kawelo, "that you are not swallowed head and tail by the shark. He has not had breakfast yet."

"We will not become the shark's breakfast," boasted the boys.

"We will be very careful," the girls said with little shivers of fear.

They continued on to the sea.

"He is a very cheerful man, that farmer," said one.

"He worries too much, though. He always warns us against the shark."

They reached the sea and forgot all about Kawelo and his warning as they plunged into the caressing waves to swim and surf.

Soon after the youngsters had gone out of sight, Kawelo stood up. "Aye," he said, "the shark has not yet had breakfast!"

He walked to the seashore and, from a hiding place in the dunes, stared out over the beach. He saw with great satisfaction that the fishermen were far out to sea in their canoes, the women were absorbed in weaving fine mats of lau hala, and the youngsters had already forgotten his warning and were surfing in the waves, the daring ones already quite far out, ripe fruit for the jaws of the shark.

Kawelo untied his kīhei, laying bare the secret that the morning breeze had tried to show the people of Mānā. Kawelo was, in truth, a being who could assume any one of four hundred different forms at will. His favorite form was that of the huge shark of never-ending appetite. He was, indeed, more shark than anything else, for when he assumed a man's form, he still bore on his back the mouth of the shark. These sharp teeth and gaping jaws were concealed by the kīhei he now tossed aside. Kawelo slipped across the beach and plunged into the water. Immediately the man changed into a shark. The huge, dangerous fish dove deep into the water until it reached its ocean home.

Kawelo looked up through the pale green water to where the children played in the surf. Soon he saw one especially daring boy swim far out from the shore. Like a lightning bolt, Kawelo shot up from his home and, opening his mouth wide, caught the boy in his jaws. The monster laughed to see the faces of all the children frozen with fear as the boy's frightened scream told them of the danger they had seen too late.

Time and again the shark found a victim, sometimes a fisherman who dove from his canoe, sometimes a woman who cooled herself in the ocean, sometimes an unwary youngster intent upon the waves. The people of Mānā grew afraid and stayed away from the ocean but Kawelo, working in his 'uala fields, was not impatient. Soon the men would go back out to sea and the women would go back to whiten their lauhala mats on the sand, and the youngsters would return to surf. Then Kawelo would eat again.

And then one day as the people of Mānā grieved for the loss of another youngster to the jaws of the shark, the people of Mānā became angry.

"How long must this senseless killing go on?" one woman demanded. "We must do something." In her voice was a reproach that stung the Mānā men.

"We will kill the shark," said the fishermen. So they went out in their canoes searching for the huge shark while the women and children watched from the shore.

There was no one left in the village to hear the laughter of Kawelo, the farmer who worked beside the path that led to the sea. "Fools!" he jeered. "I will not go into the sea while you are there with your hooks and your spears."

After many days, the people of Mānā ceased searching for the shark. "We have not seen it for many days," they assured one another. "It has gone from this place. It will not come again." And they went back to their old ways, fishing, weaving, surfing.

The patient, hungry shark ate again.

Then the people of Mānā knew they must find and destroy this shark. The waters would not be safe until this was done. "We must go to the kahuna," they said. "He will tell us what to do."

So the people of Mānā gathered together a large pig, some chickens, fish, and sea urchins, and sweet potatoes. They carried these to the heiau at Polihale and laid them at the feet of the kahuna kilokilo. "Help us!" they begged. "Tell us how to rid ourselves of this monster who eats us at his pleasure."

The priest sent two young fishermen back to their beach to bring him water fresh from the place the shark swam. He poured this water into a calabash and placed a kilo pōhaku into it, a polished stone that gave off reflections when placed under water. The priest gazed steadily at the shifting images reflected from the stone.

First he saw a large shark opening his jaws wide to display rows of sharp teeth. The kahuna nodded. It was not just a large shark that had learned to like the flesh of humans. It was a kupua, a being of supernatural powers.

Next the kahuna saw a rectangular piece of tapa fluttering in the wind, snapping and whipping back and forth in a constantly repeating motion. This was followed by the image of a small fish, then by a sweet potato vine with heart-shaped leaves. The image of the night sky came and one star shone brighter than the others.

The shark's image came again, but the shark's form changed with greater and greater speed, from shark to worm, worm to moth, from caterpillar to butterfly, from rat to man, images changing so quickly the kahuna could not follow them all. He did not need to, for he knew now how to help the people of Mānā.

The images faded and once again there was only a shiny rock in a bowl of water. The kahuna kilikilo gathered words to tell the people of Mānā how to rid themselves of the shark. This was no ordinary shark, but one that could assume many forms. It would not be easy to destroy such a being who could transform itself into so many different shapes. The identity of this kupua was clear: the tapa fluttering in a motion called kāwelowelo; the fish of a species called kawelo; the heart-shaped sweet potato vine named kawelo-kupa; the star named Kawelo-lani. There was no doubt.

The kahuna said, "The shark you seek does not live in the sea. He lives on land surrounded by 'uala vines. His name is Kawelo."

The people murmured in astonishment. "Kawelo? The farmer who speaks so pleasantly to us?"

"Does he not warn you all of the shark? The shark who has not yet had breakfast!" the kahuna said.

The people agreed that it was so. Their amazement turned to anger. "We shall go kill him."

"Wait!" ordered the kahuna sternly. Listen to my words and do not forget them. First, weave a net, a strong net to catch and hold the shark. Second, weave this net with meshes so small the feet of a butterfly will be tangled in it. Third, place the net in the sea and anchor each end to a strong tree. The shark will dive into the sea and tangle himself in the net. Pull him onto the shore, no matter what form he takes. Then, place him in an imu, heated to redness, and pile more firewood on top. Keep the fire burning for five times ten days. When this is done, cover the ashes with dry dirt. Then this monster will never bother the people of Mānā again."

The people rushed back to their village and excitedly wove a large net. It was a strong net of olonā fibers and had a very small mesh, small enough to catch and hold a tiny insect. When the net was done, they placed it in the sea and anchored the ends to strong trees on the shore. The fishermen paddled their canoes along the net, beating the water as though they were scaring large schools of fish into it. The women waded into the water holding the net as though they were swimming beside it. The youngsters and children swam and played and shouted in the surf.

Kawelo, hearing this noise, went down to the beach and looked out with increasing pleasure.

"They play and fish and swim without thought of death," he murmured. "And I am hungry. Fools that they are! The shark has not had breakfast yet!"

Swiftly he threw aside his kīhei and ran across the burning sands. Cleanly he dove into a breaker and the man changed into a huge shark. Down into the blue-green water he swam, aiming for his home in the sea where he could watch the foolish people of Mānā above him and make his choice of the most tempting morsel for his appetite.

The shark, now at full speed, smashed against the net. The fishermen yelled fiercely and struck the water with their paddles. The women and youngsters began to pull at the ends of the net and slowly the area circled by the net grew smaller and smaller. The shark, confused by the noise, fought the net with all his strength but the net held. He tried to tear at the net with rows of sharp teeth, but the finely woven fibers did not give way. Slowly he was being dragged to the beach. Kawelo changed into a fish and tried to swim below the net, but the net was large and dragged along the sand too tightly. He tried to jump over the net but the fishermen saw him and raised the net up and Kawelo fell back. He changed to a sea slug and sank to the bottom, hoping the net would slide over him, but it did not. Kawelo was angry now and changed back to his shark form and lunged at one fisherman after another, hoping to scare him into dropping his share of the net so Kawelo could swim over it into the open sea. But the water was too shallow now and his great size was of little use to him.

Then the shark turned back to a man, to Kawelo, the farmer of the sweet potatoes. "Do not hurt me," he cried out. "I am Kawelo, your neighbor!"

One man laughed. "I can see the shark's mouth on your back!" he said. "You may be Kawelo, but you are also the shark who has eaten too many of us. Now it is your turn to die!"

Quickly all the people of Mānā pulled on the net and the huge shark lay panting on the beach. Kawelo turned himself into a butterfly and rose in the air with fiercely beating wings, but a woman tossed some net over him and the mesh was so small it caught the insect's feet and the butterfly fell back to the sand.

Then Kawelo turned back to the huge shark he was, still dangerous and angry. His teeth gnashed and tore at fingers holding the net. His tail lashed with great speed and people were knocked off their feet. But in spite of all his thrashing, the giant shark was dragged across the beach.

The people threw Kawelo into the large imu they had dug and filled with stones heated to redness. They tossed in more wood and for five times ten days they kept the fire burning. At the end of this time, only gray ashes remained at the bottom of the imu. The people rejoiced to think of Kawelo dead. Now the sea was theirs to play in without fear of danger! They rushed back to the beach to enjoy themselves. The imu remained uncovered.

A kupua is not easily killed for it holds power beyond the imagining of people. That night the dark clouds gathered and a heavy rain came, filling the streams and marshes to overflowing. Kawelo, with the last of his superhuman power, had summoned this rain. The water crept into the imu, filling it. On the flood crest that flowed from the imu to the sea floated the gray ashes, all that remained of Kawelo.

As the ashes reached the sea, each particle changed into a little gray shark. Kawelo, the large shark was gone, but in his places were thousands of little sharks.

Joyfully the people went down to the sea in the morning. But when they looked out over the ocean, they could see countless little sharks swimming about. The ocean was just as dangerous as it had ever been.

In despair, the people of Mānā returned to the kahuna kilokilo at Polihale.

"Fools!" he scolded. "Didn't I tell you to fill the imu with dry dirt when the burning was through? Had you done that you would have no sharks in your waters. Now there is nothing I can do."

From then on, whenever the people passed the overgrown farm of Kawelo, they sadly remembered the words of Kawelo's warning: "Look to it as you play that you are not swallowed head and tail by the shark. He has not yet had breakfast!"

And the people of Mānā knew that when they reached the shore, they would find countless little sharks swimming in the breakers, none of which had had enough breakfast.

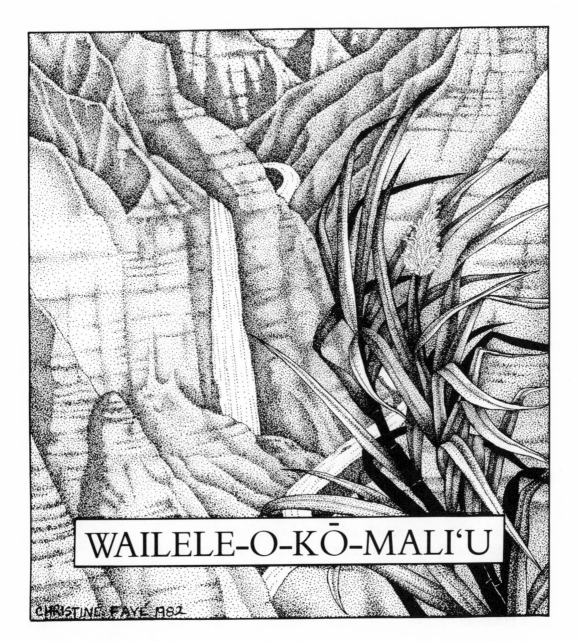

WAILELE-O-KŌ-MALIʻU

CHRISTINE FAYE 1982

WAILELE-O-KŌ-MALIʻU

When the Hawaiians first came to Kauai, they settled on the sandy plains beside a river that flowed from the high mountains down a deep canyon to the sea. There were better places for wet farming, but dry land taro grew here as did other plants that could be clumped in and around the houses and watered by bringing calabashes of water from the river. Wet land taro was grown farther up the river on the other side, reached by canoes. The river water was good to drink and so clear it was easy to find the fresh water shrimp hiding among the rocks. In front of the village stretched the shallow seas where fish swam in huge schools.

The people of this village were content for there was more than enough food. They were led by a man they all trusted for he was always fair in settling disputes. Above all, they were proud of the chief's daughter, Kō-maliʻu.

It was Kō-maliʻu who had first planted the kō-kea, the white sugar cane. It was she who had shown the farmers how to cut the top of the stalk into pieces and plant them in clumps along the edges of fields where rocks were piled up by the farmers. It was Kō-maliʻu who showed the villagers how to strip the tough outer bark from the cane and chew the sweet fibers, giving a delicious taste to the mouth as the teeth were cleaned.

Kō-maliʻu had traveled to other parts of the island to ask for information about the kō. She learned that sugar cane can be toasted over a fire and the juice squeezed out to feed babies whose mothers could no longer feed them. She taught boys and girls how to take the flower stalks and use them as darts. In this game, the darts were thrown underhand along the ground, up a slight incline with such speed that the dart would fly far and free. The dart that flew the farthest was the winner. Kō-maliʻu also brought back several species of kō, the pili-mai which could be used to make a love potion, and the laukona whose juices could be used to ward off an unwanted love potion.

Kō-maliʻu rose with the sun and worked throughout the day, looking after the affairs of the women and children, the elderly and the sick. She, too, brought calabashes of water to feed the thirsty plants and always found time to play a game of cat's cradle as she sat with friends in the shade of a tree on a hot afternoon.

The village stretched from the steep cliff on the north to the sandy beach on the south, and from the river on the east to the edge of the marshlands on the west. Each family home had six houses surrounded by a wall of stone with food plants growing wherever there was space. Pigs and dogs wandered freely about the farm-lands and houses. These animals were used as food and as guardians, for they made loud noises whenever strangers approached. Chickens, too, scratched and clucked throughout the village. It was a busy place and the inhabitants felt contented, knowing their affairs were in the hands of their wise chief and his daughter Kō-maliʻu.

From time to time a canoe bearing a chief would land on the beach, the chief having come from Oʻahu or Molokaʻi or Maui or even Hawaiʻi to seek a wife. The women of Kauai were noted for their high rank, their beauty, and their industriousness. Chiefs would come to seek Kō-maliʻu in marriage, showing off their physical skills by dodging spears thrown at them, wrestling, and performing other warlike skills all chiefs had to know. A priest would chant the genealogy of the young chief to show that he came of good lineage. The chief himself would speak of his homeland and of his ideas of responsibility and make promises he thought Kō-maliʻu would like to hear. But Kō-maliʻu, although always pleasant and courteous, sent them all away again.

Kō-maliʻu's life continued its daily round. She was unaware when eyes began to watch her from the top of the ridge behind the village, dark fierce eyes of a man nicknamed Manō, the shark.

Manō lived far up the Koaiʻe canyon. He was recklessly brave and liked to show off his strength and agility by doing foolish and dangerous stunts. He lived in a little cave behind a waterfall far above the canyon floor. Those fearful and easily impressed saw how far up it was and whispered that only birds could fly there. Tales were told of actually seeing him turn into a bird and fly off to his cave home. Because Manō liked to catch young women by surprise, he learned to move silently and swiftly, and whispers began that said he could turn himself into a rat and creep unseen into any house. He was called Manō, shark, for like the shark he liked young women, yet lived alone, no good as a husband.

When Manō heard about Kō-maliʻu, he crept down the canyon ridges to peer into the village. Kō-maliʻu was a young woman, and that was enough for Manō. He watched patiently and made his plans.

Manō went to Oʻahu where he hired some men and a canoe and stole a few things from a chief's storehouse. One day he appeared off the coast and landed his canoe. As was proper, the local warriors lined up along the beach to greet the chiefly newcomer by throwing spears at him, the short spears that are thrown underhand and the long spears that are thrown overhand. Manō dodged and parried the spears as they came, proving by his agility that he was well trained in the martial arts. He was greeted warmly by the chief.

"I have come to ask for your daughter Kō-maliʻu in marriage," Manō said.

"It is not easy to do, for many have come before you and all have left alone," the chief replied.

The young man grinned. He boasted, "I do not give up easily."

"Be welcome then," said the chief, "to try your luck." He was rather impressed with the young chief from Oʻahu who was tall and lean with broad shoulders and certainly had handled himself well at the greeting on the beach. His chiefly insignias were of good quality, too.

In the days that followed his arrival, Manō did everything he could to win the chief's affection. He paid courteous attention to Kō-maliʻu and in all ways tried to impress her. No chief had been so willing to help in the duties of the village, no chief had been better in the hunt in the mountains, for Manō seemed to know by instinct where his prey would run to ground. Surely such success was a sign of pleasure from the gods.

No warrior had shown himself better at the rough and tumble form of boxing that served as physical training for soldiers as well as a pleasurable pasttime. Manō could duck and parry, grasp and throw his opponents to the ground with great ease. He was also very apologetic each time some adversary broke an arm or a leg in the excitement of the game. All in all, the chief came to like Manō very much and was quite ready to accept the young man as his son by marriage.

One evening the chief said to his daughter, "Manō is a very fine man. He is a good warrior."

"Yes," she agreed, "he likes the martial arts very much."

"He is a very brave man," the chief pointed out. "When we are hunting he takes great risks."

"Yes," Kō-maliʻu said. "I've heard. The stories he tells get better with each retelling."

"He is wealthy and a great chief in his homeland," the chief reminded his daughter.

"So he says," she replied, for she had heard nothing except what the warrior himself had said.

"He will make a good husband," the chief said.

"No, father," Kō-maliʻu said. "He may be a well-trained warrior and brave and fearless and be truly a wealthy and great chief. However, he is a cruel man and I have seen that cruelty often in his eyes. He enjoys hurting other people and likes breaking bones. I will not have him for my husband."

She recognized the man named Manō for what he was and knew he was a dangerous man who would not make a good husband. But she also knew that Manō had dazzled her father with his willingness to help, his great strength and bravery. She saw that her father liked Manō as he had liked no other chief who had come before. She did not want to hurt her father's feelings or to openly defy him and lose his respect and love.

"I know you like this man," she told her father. "I do not. But we have not yet heard his genealogical chant. We don't know his true rank yet. Tomorrow night, let's have our priests exchange our family chants. If his family has a rank equal to ours, I will reconsider my decision not to marry him."

"Agreed," said the chief and went to alert Manō of the coming event. Manō greeted the news with a show of great pleasure. Kō-maliʻu, he intimated to everyone, would be his when she heard his rank and family tree. A celebration was called for and all the villagers were invited to join him for a pleasurable evening.

Everyone ate and drank and danced and enjoyed themselves. All too soon, everyone grew sleepy and wandered off to sleep, even those men who should have been on guard during the night.

By the time the stars had climbed halfway across the sky, everyone was sound asleep. Manō smiled wickedly. When the old chief had told him to prepare the family chant, Manō had realized at once the game was lost. He did not have a chant and it was not possible to make one up. Priests were trained to know all the genealogical chants, which were not very long since the great canoes from Kahiki had come so few generations before. He would be shown up as an imposter. There was nothing now for him to do except take by force what he had not been able to win by guile. Therefore, the guests at his table had been given food mixed with herbs that made them sleep soundly.

Carefully and silently, Manō crept into the chief's compound and went into the women's sleeping quarters. There he found Kō-maliʻu asleep, wrapped in soft, fragrant sheets of tapa. Manō lifted her gently in his arms and carried her out of the compound, out of the village, and up into the depths of Koaiʻe canyon.

At sunrise he reached his home, the little cave far up the canyon wall behind a waterfall. Usually there was not much water falling, but that night there had been heavy rains at Waiʻaleʻale and the water flowed in a cascade of noise. A spray of water splashed Kō-maliʻu on the face and she woke up.

Kō-maliʻu looked about her in confusion. She was in a moss-lined cave, not in her own sleeping house. Across the opening of the cave a sheet of falling water kept her from seeing out. Beside her was the cruel Manō. She looked into his eyes and did not like what she saw there.

"Where am I?" she demanded in a strong voice.

"Far up the Koaiʻe," Manō replied. "I need to talk to you where we will not be interrupted."

She gestured to indicate she had no choice. "Speak then."

"I wish to marry you," he said. Over the past few weeks the more she had ignored him, the more he wanted her.

"I know that," she replied. "And you know how I feel."

"That is because you do not know me," he said. "Tell me you will be my wife and I shall take you immediately back to your father so that we may celebrate our marriage."

"No," she said, "I will not marry you."

He took her by the elbow and led her to the mouth of the cave. Lifting the war club he carried, he thrust it into the water, separating its flow so that Kō-maliʻu could look out into the wilderness of the canyon. "You cannot go back without me to show the way," he said.

She looked at him. "Nothing you say can make me marry you," she said. "I will find my own way home."

Manō lifted his war club over her head threateningly. "Kō-maliʻu," he said with anger trembling in his voice, "you will agree to be my wife or I will kill you here and now."

"No," she replied.

Manō hit her with his war club and she fell. Blood flowed from her and seeped along the rocks and into the waterfall. A red ribbon sped down the stream and spread, staining the water until the stream was red from bank to bank. Manō watched and knew his crime would not be concealed and he fled to the swamps to hide. The reddish water flowed down the length of the river, hiding the shrimp on the bottom, warning the village below of some terrible deed.

The chief followed the red to its source and there behind the waterfall he found the body of his daughter. He ordered that Manō should be hunted down and killed for his crime. He returned in grief to the village bringing his daughter's body with him. He named the waterfall, calling it Wailele-o-Kō-maliʻu, Kō-ma-liʻu's Waterfall. He named the river, the canyon, and his village Waimea, Red Water, in memory of his daughter Kō-maliʻu, wise in the use of sugar cane.

KA-LAU-HE'E

Her parents named her Loli when she was born for she reminded them of the sea cucumber that lives on the reef. The loli is mottled in patches of brown and red and so was the face and body of the infant girl. "She looks like a sea cucumber," her father said in disgust, "like the loli-mākoko, the blood red sea cucumber that is good for nothing." It is true that the loli was eaten in times of famine, but not the loli-mākoko for it is bitter to the taste. Loli's parents knew, for they were lazy people and would gather and eat anything that took little effort to catch and prepare.

Loli had many brothers and sisters, but her father's taro land was small and he was lazy, expecting his children to fend for themselves. The mischievous child, the bold, saucy one could steal or snatch enough to eat, but Loli, knowing only contempt from those who should have given her affection, was a shy child. Often she would have to leave the house to search for food for herself, fern and berry and root in the uplands of Wainiha, 'opihi and crab and seaweed from the reef. She was always alone. Other children made fun of her mottled face.

"Loli! Loli!" they'd call in singsong voice, "good for nothing!" and Loli would run and hide and cry.

There was no one in Wainiha valley who cared about this infant as she grew into a child. She learned quickly that she could sit quietly under a hala and watch the women pound wauke bark into tapa. She could sit under kukui trees and watch men plant taro and sweet potatoes. Loli watched and observed and learned. She learned that people were bound together by strands of affection and she knew no one cared at all for her. Then tears of loneliness fell down her cheeks.

Sometimes the neighbors, tired of being spied upon, would tease Loli's parents about their mottle-faced daughter. Then her father would rush home and grab her and shake her and slap her. Loli never cried out but went limp in his hands like a boneless fish. Then her father would fling her away. "Just like the loli," he said disgustedly, "completely boneless. Good for nothing."

One day after the father had satisfied his anger and Loli lay on the ground where he had flung her, the mother looked at her weeping daughter. She was no longer a child. It would not be long before Loli would be a woman and married. The mother snorted. Who would marry this mottle-faced loli-mākoko? Who indeed!

"Enough!" the mother said in exasperation. "If you were busy, you'd have no time to stare at people, seeing what they do. If you were busy, you'd earn the food you eat. You must make yourself useful." The woman looked at the ugly child and thought of many things that needed to be done, but she did not want Loli around the house where she could be seen.

After much thought, the woman said, "You must make our tapa. You must plant the wauke and tend it and strip the bark and soak it and pound it into soft tapa for us to wear. Now go and begin your work."

Every morning Loli would leave her home as the sun caressed the tips of the mountain ridges with golden tendrils. She walked far up Wainiha valley, beyond the lands used by farmers. Here she planted her grove of wauke plants. She cleared away the grasses and stones and dug the earth. She knew where the farmers had thrown away their wauke roots after the harvest and she took these and planted them, watering them with her lonely tears. Loli planted the wauke in straight rows and tilled the land and pulled the weeds and brought water from the river to the new plants. As the wauke grew, she picked the tender side-shoots so that the bark would be smooth and without holes. She never neglected placing an offering to Maikoha, the man who had turned into the first wauke plant as he lay dying. She would offer a prayer to him: "No one loves me, oh Maikoha, not even my mother and father. I am alone with these my wauke plants. Let them grow tall and straight."

Her prayer touched Maikoha and he made the wauke grow tall and straight.

When the top of the wauke trees had grown twice her height, Loli cut the trees down. Carefully she peeled the bark from each tree and tied them into bundles which she carried down the valley to a little stream that joins the broad Wainiha river before it enters the ocean. She wrapped each bundle in ti leaves and placed it in the stream to soak. Loli liked this spot for here she could watch the fishermen launch their canoes and watch the children playing on the beach and hear the women on the other side of the river where they pounded their tapa. Loli was far enough away so the people of Wainiha could forget she was there and not tease and torment her, but she could still watch and observe and learn.

Here Loli built a little shelter for herself where she could store her few tools and morsels of food. And when the wauke had soaked long enough, she left an offering to Lauhuki, the daughter of Maikoha, who had taught women the art of pounding wauke bark into soft sheets of cloth. Loli never forgot to offer a prayer to her: "Oh, Lauhuki, no one helps me, not even my mother and father. Let these strips of bark join together as I beat them to form tapa." Then Loli carefully scraped off the hard outer portion of the bark and massaged the inner part until it became soft and pliable. Then she took up her beater and beat the bark, adding strip to strip until it formed a large sheet of tapa.

Her lonely prayer touched Lauhuki and the goddess made the wauke bind together into the softest and strongest tapa imaginable.

Loli then washed the tapa in the ocean and spread it in the sun to dry and bleach. She returned to her shelter and brought out the dyes, the red that comes from the kukui bark, the brown from the sap of the pala'ā fern, the yellow from the 'ōlena plant, and the black from the bark of the 'ōhi'a-hā tree. She made an offering to La'ahana, the daughter of Maikoha, the sister of Lauhuki, who had taught women the art of making patterns on tapa. Loli would pray: "Oh, La'ahana, no one teaches me, not even my mother and father. Teach me to make these sheets of tapa become beautiful in design." And she would color in the designs she had seen on the reefs and in the sea, the sea urchin's spiny roundness, the markings on the turtle's back, the intricate designs of the cowry shells.

Her prayers touched La'ahana and the goddess made sure the designs were lovely to see.

When the tapa was finished, Loli took it home to give to her mother. Loli could make a tapa a day and soon her family grew rich indeed, for the wealth of a family was often counted in the number and quality of its fine tapa that could be given to friends and family and sent as gifts to the chiefs. No tapa in Wainiha or even in the entire district of Hanalei was more finely made, more beautiful to look at. But no one learned to love Loli because of the beautiful tapa she made. Instead people were jealous and went out of their paths to tease and torment her all the more, and women even began to put their bundles of wauke in the stream where Loli soaked hers. But they did not talk to her and invite her to join them as they beat their tapa in company. So Loli continued her lonely life.

But Maikoha and his daughters Lauhuki and La'ahana had learned to love her for no one else offered them such heart-felt prayers for their gifts. They wished to ease her loneliness and went to Ka-he'e-hauna-wela, god of the squid and octopus, to ask him to help them with their plan.

And so it was that one day, as Loli sat on a rock in her stream scraping the wauke bark, she noticed a he'e swimming near her. It was a large squid, mottled in shades of red and brown over its body. Loli looked at it in astonishment for it was a he'e-mākoko that lives in the deep ocean.

"You are from the deep sea," she told the he'e, "and do not belong in this brackish water. Come, swim into this bowl and I will return you to your home."

Carefully carrying the he'e in her bowl, she waded across the river and across the sand to bring the he'e to the sea. The he'e swam away slowly. The fishermen taunted Loli as she stood at the sea's edge. "Be careful, Loli!" they called. "Our nets are empty. We may catch you and that squid for our supper tonight! But no," the men told each other, "they are both mākoko and too bitter to eat. Good for nothing!" Their cruel laughter brought fresh tears to Loli's eyes as she returned to her lonely shelter under the kukui trees beside the little stream where her bundles of wauke soaked.

Soon she noticed the he'e again swimming near her. "What, are you back?" she said in surprise. The mottled squid swam nearer. "Why," she said, "I think you are as lonely as I am. Come sit beside me and we shall talk together."

The he'e climbed up onto a small rock at the edge of the stream and watched with interest as Loli's busy fingers scraped strip after strip of outer bark from the wauke. Loli, knowing she could not be teased by the squid and glowing in the warmth of an intent listener, poured out the story of her brief life. Evening came. The he'e slipped from the rock and followed the stream out to sea. Loli went home empty-handed for she had not beaten the strips into tapa. She went to sleep hungry, for her parents would not feed her, but happy.

Day after day, when she came down from her upland wauke patches, Loli found the he'e waiting in the stream and called to him to join her. Hour after hour she would sit beside him, now talking, now resting in comfortable silence, as she made her tapa.

"You are my only friend," she told the he'e. In time Loli felt a love for the squid for he proved to be a faithful companion to her. At last she turned to her friend and said, "I do not know why you come here to listen to me. And yet I thank you for I have come to love you."

The he'e slipped into the water near the soaking tapa and jetted out a cloud of black dye. From the inky waters rose a young man, his face and body mottled like that of Loli.

"Do not be afraid," the young man said. "I have often watched your tears, and great love has filled my heart for you."

"No one can love me," said Loli unhappily. "I am too ugly. Even my parents say that."

"Look at me," said the young man gently. "We are very much alike."

Loli looked and joyously went into the embrace of his open arms. The hours went by as the tapa soaked in the inky waters unheeded.

When Loli returned home, she gave the piece of tapa to her mother.

"What is this?" exclaimed the mother angrily. "Look at this tapa! It is soft and mushy. No one can use it for anything. You have soaked it in the water too long. Ugly girl, you grow too careless." And the mother crumpled up the tapa into a small bundle and threw it at Loli. "Eat that if you are hungry. Wrap yourself in it if you are cold. You will not eat or sleep in this house tonight."

And every day, Loli went from the house of her parents taking a piece of tapa with her to wash in the stream. And each day when she returned home, the tapa was soft and slimy, soaked too long, unheeded in the inky waters.

At last her mother grew alarmed. "Something has happened to that girl," she told her husband. "I don't know what she does down there by that stream, but I will find out."

So the next day, when Loli went from the house early in the morning, her mother followed her carefully so that Loli would not see her. Loli's mother watched the girl put the tapa into the water and heard her call out, "He'e, beloved, where are you?"

Horrified, the mother watched as the he'e came, squirted out its black ink, and appeared as a young man. He was as ugly as her daughter, but nonetheless a young man. The mother watched the two embrace and wander off among the trees while the tapa soaked in the water.

In great haste, the mother returned home and told her husband what she had seen. When Loli returned to the house that evening, her parents caught her and bound her with rope.

"Why do you tie me?" cried the girl. "You are hurting me."

"Ugly girl, to bring such disgrace upon our family," her father said in cold anger.

"Taking up with every young man that comes by," her mother said, "even with a beast from the sea."

"He loves me," cried the girl. "No one else has ever loved me. And I love him. I want to live with him and be his wife."

"Never!" cried her parents. "You cannot be wife to a demi-god of the sea, a being who is part-man, part-squid."

"I love him!" Loli cried in anguish.

"You will stay where you are, tied up, without food or water," her parents told her sternly. "When you have promised us that you will never see that creature again, and return to making fine tapa, we will set you free."

Bitter tears filled the eyes of the girl. "All my life you have told me I was ugly," she cried. "You named me loli-mākoko and teased me and hit me. Now when I have found someone who loves me, you tie me with rope and leave me without food and water until I give up my love. I shall never do it."

"Starve then," her parents said, shrugging their shoulders. "It is bad enough to feed you and care for you and be teased by the neighbors. But never shall you disgrace our family in such a way. This is too much."

During that night, Loli wept for her lost friend whom she had come to love very much. Her tears dropped swiftly down her cheeks and fell onto the ropes that tied her hands together. At last the fibers were so wet they loosened their grip. Fiercely, Loli worked to free herself from the ropes and they dropped from her. With a cry that woke her parents, she leapt from the house. Even in the dark of night, her feet knew the path, but her parents stumbled as they pursued her.

"Come back!" they yelled. "Come back!"

Loli ran toward the sea and ran up onto the bluff overlooking the great expanse of the ocean.

"He'e!" she called. "He'e, beloved, I come to you!"

Her parents' fingers grasped at her as Loli leapt from the bluff. Horrified, they watched her drop onto the rocks, saw her lift her head, heard her call once, "He'e!" and then lie still.

A wave came racing in towards the rocks where Loli lay unmoving. A he'e rode the crest of the wave. The ocean foamed over the rocks in a deep surge that lifted the body of the girl. On this flood of rolling water, the he‘e of the deep seas swam to Loli and gently touched her. The wave dashed against the cliff and flung itself back out into the ocean. Loli's body was no longer crushed on the rocks. Instead, out to sea two he‘e rode on the waves, their tentacles intermingling like lovers' arms.

Maikoha and his daughters were pleased with the outcome of their plan. To punish the cruel Wainiha people, they cursed the spot where Loli had soaked her wauke. Even to this day, when any clothes are washed in the little stream where it enters the Wainiha river, the fabric becomes soft and mushy, unfit for use.

This is the place that is named Ka-lau-he‘e.

KA-'ŌPELE

CHRISTINE FAYÉ 1982

KA-'ŌPELE

The heiau of Kukui was completed at Kaiki-hauna-kā on the seashore of Ka-waihau. Kukui was built for the gods, but not yet dedicated to them. Two human sacrifices were needed.

A priest sailed to O'ahu to search that island for sacrifices. He found a corpse near Wai'anae and put it into his canoe. He went on to Māeaea at Waialua and saw a man lying as one dead on the beach.

The priest asked the nearby villagers about this body. One old man replied, "We only know his name is Ka-'ōpele. But where he came from, what he did, and why he is dead on the beach of Māeaea we do not know."

The villagers gladly gave the Kauai priest permission to take Ka-'ōpele's body from their beach.

The priest returned to Kauai and placed the two bodies on the altar of Kukui. After six months, the bones of the first man had fallen apart and lay bleached and white on the altar. Strangely, the flesh of Ka-'ōpele remained firm.

One night, dark clouds gathered above Wai'ale'ale, lightning flashed, and thunder resounded from the cliffs. An earthquake shook the land, tumbling houses onto the sleeping inhabitants. Ka-'ōpele sat up on the altar. "I have slept a long time," he murmured to himself. "I lay down at Māeaea, but I don't recognize this place."

Rising from the altar, he made his way out of the heiau. Ka-'ōpele came to an old man weeping beside his fallen house. "What are you crying for, old man?" asked Ka-'ōpele.

"Pele shook the earth in her rage just now," was the reply, "and my house is destroyed. I, Ka-'ulu, am too old now and there is no one to help me build another."

"Don't you have any grown children to help you?" Ka-'ōpele asked.

"A son," Ka-'ulu said. "But he and his wife Nanau do not welcome me at their place. Hō'iole and Nanau never come to visit me. Only my granddaughter comes to visit when she can."

"Stop crying, old man," said Ka-'ōpele. "I'm here and I will help you rebuild your house."

"I cannot pay you," said Ka-'ulu.

"If you have a bit of food," replied Ka-'ōpele, "that will be payment enough. I have slept a long time and I'm hungry."

Ka-'ulu found a calabash of poi and some dried fish in the ruins of his home. Ka-'ōpele ate and then helped make a shelter where the old man could sleep for the rest of the night. Ka-'ōpele looked at the pieces of the fallen house and saw that none of the beams were broken, for the framework had simply come unlashed and had fallen to the ground. Quietly, so as not to disturb the old man, Ka-'ōpele began rebuilding the house.

In the morning, the old man awoke and was astonished. "You've worked hard while I slept," said Ka-'ulu.

"It's nothing," replied Ka-'ōpele. "Show me where pili grass grows and I'll make fresh thatching for your house."

Ka-'ulu led Ka-'ōpele to a wild field of pili grass and helped him cut and bundle the grass. That evening the house was completed. Lau hala mats were spread on the floor and calabashes hung on posts out of reach of rats.

"All day I've been thinking how to thank you," Ka-'ulu said. "Answer one question for me. Do you have a wife?"

"If I have a wife, she has forgotten me," said Ka-'ōpele.

"Good," Ka-'ulu said. "I'll bring my granddaughter to you. Her name is Ka-hala because she is expert at weaving lau hala. She works from dawn to dusk and as hard as you do. She will make a fine wife for you."

"You've fed me, old man," said Ka-'ōpele. "That is thanks enough."

"No, no," replied Ka-'ulu. "Wait here and I will bring my granddaughter so you two can meet."

Ka-'ulu hurried off to find his granddaughter. While he was away, Ka-'ōpele tilled the land around the old man's house and planted banana trees, sweet potato vines, and corms of dry land taro. While doing this, he heard a great commotion coming from the heiau. Drums boomed, conch shells trumpeted, and people shouted. From time to time the noise stopped and a priest shouted out the good news: "The gods have accepted our sacrifice! They left the bones of one man, but took the entire body of the other. Great is the power of our gods!"

Ka-'ōpele smiled to himself. He was thankful the priest had not put a knife into his heart and ended his life while he slept.

Meanwhile the old man reached his son's house. He told Ka-hala about the man who was helping him. "He's tall and handsome, too," he said, "and very industrious. He will make a good husband for you."

"Go away," Hō'iole said angrily. "Don't tease my daughter with such non-sense. There is a chief from the Kona district who wants to marry her. She'll marry him."

"A chief's love for a commoner is as short as the day," quoted Ka-'ulu. "You'd do well, granddaughter, to marry Ka-'ōpele instead."

"I'll come with you and meet him," Ka-hala said.

Nanau, watching her daughter with bitter eyes, said to Hō'iole, "The Kona chief is a better match for her than this man. Stop them." But there was nothing they could do, for the girl and her grandfather left the house, paying no attention to the protests of Hō'iole and Nanau.

After a time, Ka-hala and Ka-'ōpele decided to marry. Her parents muttered, "After the wedding, come back to our place. Your husband has no land of his own, so he might as well work for us."

Ka-'ōpele and Ka-hala lived with her grandfather, but Ka-'ōpele farmed the land of her parents as well. The first night they were together, when his wife fell asleep, Ka-'ōpele went to the farmlands. He tilled the ground and planted sweet potatoes, taro, bananas, wauke, sugar cane, and all other useful plants.

When she awoke that first morning, Ka-hala was alarmed over his absence. She looked this way and that way and could not find him. Finally, worried, she asked her parents, "Have you seen my husband this morning?"

"Is he gone already?" Nanau asked scornfully. "That didn't last long!"

Just then Ka-hala saw Ka-'ōpele coming down the path from the mountains. "Where have you been?" she asked. "Didn't you realize I'd worry about you? Next time take me with you."

Ka-'ōpele replied, "The son of a chief can sleep until the sun is overhead and find food already cooked for him when he gets up. But a common man must cultivate the soil and must gather food where it can be found. You must not worry, for I'll always come back."

The next morning when Ka-hala awoke she again missed her husband. Soon she saw him climbing the path from the sea, laden down with a great quantity of fish. "I have been fishing," he replied to her scoldings. "A chief may awake in the morning and find fish waiting in his fishing ponds, but a common man must catch his own fish."

Although his parents-in-law ate well on the food Ka-'ōpele grew and on the fish he caught, they still grumbled. "Our daughter was loved by a Kona chief," they said. "We could have been wrapped in feather cloaks now if she had married him."

Day after day Ka-hala awoke to find her husband gone from the house. At last, one night as they sat in their home, she said to him, "Do you never sleep, my husband? It seems to me you are always working and never rest."

Ka-'ōpele took his wife in his arms. "Listen to me," he said. "Ever since I was a little boy I have not slept like other men. I stay awake for twelve months at a time and then I fall into a trance-like sleep for six months. You have heard," he continued, "the priest of Kukui heiau tell of the disappearance of a man's body sacrificed on the altar. I am that man. I was found asleep on the beach at Māeaea on O'ahu and was brought to Kauai. When the thunder and lightning came with the earthquake, I woke up. Soon I shall sink again into a sleep. It is a sleep that approaches death. But I will not be dead. Guard my body and in six months I shall awaken and can hold you in my arms again."

"I understand," Ka-hala whispered. "I shall never forget your words. When you fall asleep I shall watch over you and will long for the day you will wake up again."

Ka-'ōpele and Ka-hala lived happily together until one day he returned home and lay down on the lauhala mats. His breathing deepened and then lessened until it could not be heard. His wife, pressing her ear against his chest, heard his heart beat grow softer and softer until she could no longer hear it. She spread a soft tapa over her sleeping husband.

"Sleep well," she murmured. "I didn't have time to tell you that we are going to have a baby."

After several days had gone by, Hō'iole and Nanau came, ready to complain because they had not gotten fresh food from Ka-'ōpele. "What is this?" Hō'iole said when he saw Ka-'ōpele stretched out on his bed. "Why is he sleeping instead of feeding our hungry stomachs?" He entered the house and shook Ka-'ōpele's shoulder. He peered closely and then said, "This man is dead."

"He is asleep," Ka-hala said. "He's not dead."

"We shall see," Hō'iole said. He got a small calabash and filled it with water. He held it below Ka-'ōpele's nostrils. "No breath disturbs the water," Hō'iole said. He laid his ear against his son-in-law's chest. "There is no heart beat. This man is dead."

"He's only asleep, I tell you," Ka-hala said.

"Poor girl," Nanau said pityingly. "You can't tell the difference between death and sleep. We must bury this man."

"You shall not bury Ka-'ōpele. He's not dead!" Ka-hala said angrily.

Hō'iole shook his head. "You must hold our daughter," he told Nanau. "She's raving. You must tie her up so I can get rid of the body in peace."

Nanau held Ka-hala while her father carried the body of Ka-'ōpele away. Ka-hala fought fiercely against her mother's grasp. "He's asleep! He's asleep!" she cried.

Hō'iole tied stones around Ka-'ōpele's ankles, then wrapped the body with koali vines, and placing it in his canoe, paddled out to sea. He dropped Ka-'ōpele's body overboard and it quickly sank out of sight into the deep water.

"Now we can send for the Kona chief to marry you!" Nanau said. "You will be a chiefess."

"I am the wife of Ka-'ōpele and the mother of his child," she told her parents. "I will have nothing to do with this Kona chief."

Many times Ka-hala went down to gaze upon the ocean that held her husband's body. When the new life within her moved, she shed tears. "You will never see your child, Ka-'ōpele," she wept. "I shall never feel your strong arms about me again. I have only your child as a reminder of you."

Then there came a night when dark clouds piled up on Wai'ale'ale, lightning flashed and thunder resounded over the land. An earthquake shook the village and tumbled houses to the ground. Ka-hala lay in the ruins of her home as her child was born. She wrapped him in tapa and cradled him in her arms. She did not notice a man striding up the path. She only heard his angry voice lashing her. "You did not guard my body. I awoke to find myself tied with koali vines and with stones weighing down my body in the depths of the sea."

This man was dripping wet, his skin wrinkled by water, and seaweed seemed to be growing all over him. He seemed a fearful sea monster, but Ka-hala recognized him immediately. "Don't scold me, Ka-ʻōpele!" she cried. "My mother held me while my father sank your body in the sea. They would not listen to me. I would have died to join you but I could not because I was carrying your child. And see," Ka-hala said, holding the baby out to him, "Here is your son."

Tenderly Ka-ʻōpele took his son. "We shall name him Ka-leleʻa-lu-aka, the image of a dripping sea monster," he said. He put the baby down gently and covered him to protect him from the night wind. With a cry of gladness, he swept his wife into his arms. "My sleep was long," he said. "I dreamed of you and wanted to hold you in my arms again like this."

He dried her tears and when mother and child were sleeping, he rose and began to rebuild their house.

In the morning Ka-hala's parents came down the path to her home. "Our house was knocked flat . . ." Nanau began. Then she saw Ka-ʻōpele and her face blanched with fear.

"He's alive!" Nanau whispered fearfully.

"He's alive!" Hōʻiole shouted and they ran far into the mountains to hide. They never came again to interrupt the lives of Ka-hala and Ka-ʻōpele.

Ka-ʻōpele and Ka-hala lived happily together. When sleep overtook him, she guarded his body. Their son, Ka-leleʻa-lu-aka, grew strong and tall and became famous throughout the islands of Hawaiʻi. When death took Ka-ʻōpele and Ka-hala, they wandered hand in hand in the lands of Milu where they still dwell in happiness.

KANALOA-HULUHULU

KANALOA-HULUHULU

Strange rumors reached Kaua-hoa, carried down by chilly mountain winds. Kaua-hoa, the king's constable, heard rumors of things not being well, whispers of strange omens being heard and seen, and tales of dwarves and giants appearing again in the land.

Then a message came from the bird catchers of Kilohana, perched at the edge of Alaka'i swamp above the black cliffs of Wainiha. "We have found a man injured in Kōke'e," the message said. "Come and hear his story."

Kaua-hoa placed food in a gourd container and slung it over one shoulder and over the other slung his pīkoi, a small club tied to a cord which, when the club was thrown, encircled the opponent's arms and made him helpless. Kaua-hoa slipped on the wrist loop holding his dagger with its concave curve ending in a sharp point, a useful weapon for both thrusting and striking. He took up his long spear, which would serve him both as a weapon and as a walking stick.

He climbed the steep, narrow path beside Maunahina waterfall to Kilohana. The bird catchers met him and shook their heads sadly. "Too late," one of them said. "The man died in the dark hours of the morning, but we have kept him for you to see."

Kaua-hoa examined the man. His body was bruised, several long bones were broken, and a shoulder had been dislocated. Kaua-hoa sat back on his heels. "These wounds were caused by someone trained in lua," he said. Lua was a terrible method of hand-to-hand combat that used all the holds and tricks of wrestling and added a few special tricks of its own. Its aim was to dislocate joints and break bones so that the loser could be strangled with a noose.

"Where did you find him?" Kaua-hoa asked.

"He came here. The Kōke'e trail is dangerous. We don't go that way any more."

"Dangerous? How so?"

"We heard," the bird catcher said, and his companion nodded strongly in agreement, "that there is a giant who leaps upon travelers and takes their goods and sometimes kills them."

"A giant?" asked Kaua-hoa. "I thought they were all gone."

"Perhaps," came the reply. "I don't know. Some say he is big and very, very hairy. Others say he is short and has no hair at all. Anyway it is better not to use the trail."

"Safer for you, maybe, but it's my job to keep the trails free from danger," said Kaua-hoa. "I'm curious to see this giant. Where can I find him?"

"He lives in a grove of lehua trees in a small, boggy place, the place where travelers get lost."

Kaua-hoa nodded. He remembered that particular boggy place, heavily overgrown with trees and shrubs. It was an area large enough for someone unfamiliar with the trails to get lost in the underbrush. This was a central place in Kōke'e and many trails went through it. It was easy for a traveler to think he was on the trail to Kalalau and then, hours later, find himself looking unexpectedly down into Nu'alolo or into the deep valley of Wainiha. It was a place where one had to go slowly, so it was an ideal spot, Kaua-hoa realized, for a giant to cause trouble.

Kaua-hoa left the bird catchers and by mid-afternoon he came to the boggy grove of lehua trees. He entered the grove, making no attempt to hide his presence. If a giant there was, Kaua-hoa wanted to meet him!

A large man stepped from behind a lehua trunk and blocked the path. He was only a little taller than Kaua-hoa himself, with wide shoulders topping a strong body bulging with muscles. His arms were very long, his hands reaching his knees. He was covered with a great mass of hair that grew everywhere on his body, from his head over his chin, down his arms and torso, and over his legs.

"Where are you going?" the giant demanded.

"I've come to find you," Kaua-hoa answered. "What is your name?"

"I am called Kanaloa," the giant replied.

"Never heard of you," Kaua-hoa said. "You can't be the famous Kana who broke the turtle's back so that the mountains wouldn't grow any more." He laughed. "I shall call you Kanaloa-huluhulu, the very hairy one."

The giant flushed angrily. "No one uses this trail without my permission," he said.

"This trail was built for the use of everyone at all times," replied Kaua-hoa. "It belongs to no one person, not even an ugly, hairy fool like you." He pulled one of his eyelids down and stuck out his tongue.

Such insults were too much for the giant, more used to people pleading with him to save their lives than being defied. He raised his club and smashed it down.

The king's constable dodged the blow easily. The giant was big but his long arms took too long to deliver the blows intended to stun and kill, and so the blows were easy to avoid.

Kaua-hoa settled down on his feet like an octopus on the ocean floor with its tentacles spread out. Kanaloa rolled his club and twisted it and turned it in a strange, peculiar fashion and, when he thought Kaua-hoa was off guard, attempted to thrust it into the constable's face. If it had connected, it would have driven Kaua-hoa's nose deep into his head, like a nail into wood.

Kaua-hoa leaped up and threw a handful of dust into the giant's eyes. The giant stumbled, and dropped his club. He wove about like a person on a dark night moving on an unknown trail. Darting in quickly, Kaua-hoa grabbed the little finger of the hairy giant and twisted it until he heard the snap of a breaking bone.

The battle between the king's constable and the hairy giant raged. Trees were uprooted. Plants were torn from the ground and trampled into the bog. Birds fled from the grove to lead their busy lives in more peaceful places.

Kanaloa threw Kaua-hoa over his shoulder as though he were throwing a cloak about himself, but Kaua-hoa twisted about and fell onto the giant's back, wrapping his legs around Kanaloa's waist and his hands around the giant's neck. Kanaloa laughed and reached to pull the constable from his back. Kaua-hoa jumped away quickly. He swung his pīkoi and let it go. It wrapped around the giant's knees. Already off balance, the giant fell heavily. Kaua-hoa leaped on his back and used his dagger to cut off the giant's head.

Kaua-hoa left the giant's body there in the bog where it had fallen among the broken trees. He took the head with him and returned to Kilohana and the bird catchers. There, in the fading light, he tossed the giant's head over the cliff where it disappeared into the rocks and trees thousands of feet below.

But a giant is not so easily killed as that. He will not die until the sun sets, and will not die at all if he can put head and body back together. So it was that Kanaloa rose to his feet soon after the king's constable had left and felt along the ground with his fingers, seeking his head. Unable to find it, Kanaloa tore up the lehua trees by their roots to search in their branches and under their roots. He stamped about, crushing all the remaining trees and shrubs into the bog. He stamped up and down, searching and searching, until the ground became hard and dry. He pulled out all the plants and trampled them underfoot.

When the sun set, the body of Kanaloa lost its life and fell to the ground. Where the lehua grove had been there was nothing but a dusty plain.

This place is known as Kanaloa-huluhulu, named after the hairy giant. No tree will grow here because, it is whispered, the giant's ghost still haunts this grassy clearing, looking endlessly for his head.

LAU-HAKA

LAU-HAKA

Lau-haka had never known his mother or father, for his mother died at his birth and his father, a stranger to Wainiha valley, had gone and never returned. Once the bird catcher Kāne-'alohi, who was his mother's brother, told Lau-haka of the stranger who had descended the steep trail from the mountains, seen Lau-haka's mother bathing in a pool and taken her as his wife. Before the stranger had climbed the path again never to return, he had given her his feathered helmet. Only a chief could wear such a helmet. It became the only keepsake Lau-haka had of his mother and he kept it carefully wrapped in tapa in a large, covered gourd.

"The helmet proves your father was a chief and so you are a chief yourself," his uncle told Lau-haka.

"A helmet doesn't prove anything," Lau-haka said. "You are my father and I am a bird catcher like you, nothing more."

Lau-haka grew up at Maunahina, a Wainiha village named after the waterfall that tumbles down the black cliffs from Alaka'i swamp. His uncle Kāne-'alohi was a bird catcher and from the day of Lau-haka's birth had trained Lau-haka in the skill of trapping colorful birds whose red, yellow, and black feathers were used to make the cloaks and helmets of chiefs.

For many months of the year, Lau-haka and Kāne-'alohi lived in the lehua forests of Kōke'e. Lau-haka was taught to make the proper offerings to Kū-hulu-hulu-manu, god of the bird catchers. He learned to arouse a bird's curiosity by imitating its call. The bird would fly nearer and nearer to the strange call until it perched on one of the branches that Lau-haka had smeared with the sticky sap of the kukui tree. Then the bird, its feet stuck to the branch, could not fly away and Lau-haka caught it, plucked a few colorful feathers, and released it to regrow its lost feathers. Lau-haka learned to be very patient and could remain motionless for many hours holding a tubular flower between his finger and thumb waiting for a honey creeper to dip its beak into the flower's throat. When the honey creeper did, Lau-haka closed his fingers and caught the bird by its beak. He grew wise and cunning in the setting of traps and the catching of wary birds.

The bird catchers built a home beside a pool at the top of the cliffs where the trail that led into Wainiha began and the trail of logs across Alaka'i swamp ended. Here, along the cliff tops the 'uwa'u nested in holes they dug between the tree roots and rocks. Kāne-ʻalohi and Lau-haka caught the wild ʻuwaʻu, a large bird with a black head, white forehead, and slate-colored back. The young birds were delicious roasted over a fire while the old birds, because of their strong fishy flavor were salted down in covered calabashes for times when fresh meat was not available. The ʻuwaʻu left their nests at dawn to spend the day soaring over the ocean seeking the fish they ate. At dusk, they wearily returned to their nests. The unlucky ones never noticed the nets spread over the entrance to their holes and were easily caught. Lau-haka became adept at imitating the sounds of these birds, a long drawn out u-a-u.

The bird catchers' home was a safe haven. The trail up from Wainiha was so narrow one man could defend it easily and when anyone stepped on the log path across the swamp, the pond beside their house would ripple. Lau-haka and his uncle, as wary as birds, always knew when someone, friend or foe, was coming and they could then disappear into the swamp and forest where no one dared follow them.

"We will live in peace here," Kāne-ʻalohi said. "No one will disturb us."

Kāne-ʻalohi did not know that Hakau, the chief of Waimea, had heard of them and was very angry. Hakau was a harsh ruler and demanded death as the punishment for any wrong-doing. When he heard of the bird catchers living at the other end of Alakaʻi swamp, he demanded of his ministers, "Where is the tax these bird catchers must pay for the birds in my forest? Where are my feathers? Where is my fresh ʻuwaʻu?" But of course no-one could show him these things for the bird catchers knew nothing of Hakau's tax. The birds flew free in the forest for anyone wily enough to trap them and the feathers and meat were exchanged for poi and tapa which the bird catchers could not make for themselves.

That two bird catchers were busy in the mountains and did not fear him enough to pay tribute made Hakau angry. He ordered the captain of a troop of soldiers to bring the bird catchers to him.

The soldiers rushed to the mountains and across Alakaʻi. They did not know their passage across the swamp had caused the pond to ripple and when the soldiers reached the bird catchers' house, it was deserted.

Fearfully, the captain reported back to Hakau, empty-handed. "We destroyed their hut," he said.

"I shall have to go myself," Hakau grumbled angrily. He said to his bodyguards, "Get yourselves ready, but first take this man away and kill him."

The bodyguards locked up the captain to await his death, but during the night he escaped and fled for sanctuary over the mountain and down the Wainiha trail and beyond to a temple of refuge. As he paused before descending the Mauna-hina trail, he told Lau-haka and Kane-'alohi why their home had been destroyed and warned them of Hakau's coming.

A few days later, Lau-haka and his uncle were roasting 'uwa'u over a small fire. The young man noticed the water in the pond had started to ripple. As he watched, the ripples covered the pond completely, indicating that a sizeable group was crossing the swamp. He said to his uncle, "Tear the bird into pieces. We must eat while there is still time. The water is rippling."

Kāne-'alohi looked at the pond. "No one is coming," he said. "Those are wind ripples."

"There are dark shadows on the water," replied Lau-haka. "There are many men coming." He tore the roasting bird into pieces and the two men ate the half raw meat quickly.

When Kāne-'alohi saw the chief and his soldiers as they crested a small hill, Kāne-'alohi groaned. "So many men," he said, "and only two of us."

Lau-haka pushed his frightened uncle down the trail to a narrow place where only one man at a time could pass. On one side was black volcanic rock and on the other a drop of a thousand feet. Here Lau-haka put on his feather helmet and stood waiting. In his hands he held a long, polished stick, the only weapon he had. The soldiers had to come down the trail single file. First one man, then another fought Lau-haka but he sent each of them over the side to his death. The remaining soldiers stood paralyzed, as afraid of the man in front of them as of their chief behind them.

Hakau ordered his soldiers back and moved down the trail until the chief and the determined birdcatcher stood face to face. Lau-haka grasped his stick so he could throw it. He was no match for a highly trained warrior. He could only throw his stick, hoping to gain time, and run.

Hakau raised his hand, palm out and open to show he held no weapons at the ready. "By what right do you wear a chief's helmet?" he demanded.

"It was a gift from my father to my mother," Lau-haka answered.

"That is the helmet I left at Maunahina," Hakau said. "Are you my son?"

"Uncle!" called Lauhaka. "Look at this man. Is he my father?"

Kāne-'alohi nodded. "Yes," he said.

The chief and his son embraced and Hakau said, "I'll return to Waimea and build a special meeting house. When it's finished, I'll send for you and name you as my son. You'll be the ruling chief after me."

Hakau returned to Waimea with no intention of keeping his promise. He was angry that only one man had defeated him in battle. He was humiliated because a backwoods bird catcher had claimed him as his father, and Hakau was determined to be rid of the pest. "He's not my son," the chief told his men. "A helmet in itself doesn't prove a thing. He must have stolen it. How else could he have gotten it?"

Hakau ordered his soldiers to dig a large, deep hole and place sharpened spears in it so that anyone falling in would be impaled. Over this pit a meeting house was built and a large lauhala mat was spread over the hole. Hakau planned to seat his men so they could hold onto the edges of the mat so that it would appear to be lying directly on the ground. When the meeting house was finished, Hakau sent a message inviting Lau-haka to come to Waimea.

Lau-haka and his uncle came down the mountains to Waimea. The villagers stared at their chief's son as he strode up to take his place at his father's side. Lau-haka stopped in the doorway of the new house and saw the chief reclining on the edge of a large lau hala mat, beckoning him to enter. He looked at the soldiers lining the walls of the house. There were no weapons by them. They all sat in the same position, legs crossed, white-knuckled hands under their knees.

"I've never seen a meeting house with no one sitting in the middle," whispered Kāne-'alohi.

"Neither have I," replied Lau-haka. He threw his spear into the center of the room and with a tearing sound it pierced the mat. Anger flooded Lau-haka and he leaped into the meeting house and ran along the wall, knocking several soldiers into the pit meant for him. The unarmed men scrambled to get out of the way. The chief jumped up facing the furious young man and as Lau-haka said, "Did you really think you could kill me so easily?", the chief stepped backwards. Hakau fell into the trap he'had intended for his son.

As soon as the soldiers saw their chief die, they surrendered to Lau-haka. The bird catcher ordered them to tear down the meeting house and pile the wood in

123

the pit. Lau-haka tossed a torch on the pile, which flamed fiercely as it consumed the treacherous Waimea chief.

When the Waimea people were told of Lau-haka's parentage and of his father's treachery, they said, "Let Lau-haka be our new chief!" and happily shouted their approval.

The young man was flushed with pride. He stepped forward to accept the new role offered him.

Kāne-'alohi held him by his elbow. "Wait," he warned. "Take time to think. You are not trained to be a chief. Will you be any better than your father?"

But Lau-haka pulled his arm away and became the new chief of Waimea. Kāne-'alohi returned alone to the mountains. From time to time travelers brought him news of his nephew and not all of the news was good. Kāne-'alohi smiled and built another small house beside his own.

One day Lau-haka returned, carrying an infant son in his arms. "I am not a chief," he told Kāne-'alohi. "I am a bird catcher, nothing more. I want to teach my son to be a bird catcher too."

For the rest of their lives, the three bird catchers lived in the lehua forests trapping colorful birds and plucking a few feathers from each before letting them go again. In the evenings beside the rippling pond, Kāne-'alohi put a bird on the spit to roast. The bird catchers would tear apart the birds of Kāne-'alohi and eat, looking down into Wainiha and over the ocean where the 'uwa'u flew.

NĀ KEIKI O NĀ-ʻIWI

"Father, why can't we go down to play with the children in Kalalau?" Ku-a-pōhaku asked. He was a small boy, with the same bushy hair and eyebrows of his father. He, his father Nā-'iwi, and his sister Hiki-mauna-lei were sitting deep inside the cave that was their home. Across the cave's entrance, Nā-'iwi had placed a mat of woven banana leaves to keep out the sun's rays. The noise of children came faintly to their ears, brought to their cave above Kalalau by the winds flowing up the valley.

Nā-'iwi sat silently, his fingers continuing to mash pink-fleshed bananas into a poi for their supper.

"Why, father?" prodded Hiki-mauna-lei. She knew Nā-'iwi was a silent man and needed to be prodded to talk.

Nā-'iwi sighed. "I say you may not," he murmured without anger.

"But why?" Ku-a-pōhaku leaned forward to plant his elbow on his father's knee and stared boldly into his father's face. "We never play with the other children. We sleep during the day. They sleep during the night."

"We are the Mū people," Nā-'iwi said. "The people down there think of us as wild animals. They will hurt you."

Ku-a said, "Sometimes when my sister and I go down to trade banana for fish in the early evening, we meet some of the children who are still awake. They have not hurt us."

"We speak differently than they do," Nā-'iwi said. "Our speech sounds harsh and strange to them. They will laugh at you."

"They have not laughed," Ku-a said, "although we do not talk much. There was no time. We had our work to do, and they had to sleep."

Nā-'iwi sighed again. He placed the bowl of mashed banana between them and carefully removed bananas that had been roasting in the hot ashes of the fire. He gestured to his children to eat, but sat turned away from them, staring at the light shining through the mat at the cave's entrance.

What would life hold for them, he wondered. They were Mū, the little forest people, the silent ones. They lived in the wet upland forests, for only here could the banana be grown all year long. The banana gave food, shelter, and clothing. But now the Mū were almost all gone from the island. Most had left with the

Menehune, but a few like Nā-'iwi lived out their lives hidden in the upland forests unable to leave precious places or memories.

Nā-'iwi turned to gaze into the faces of his children. They looked so much like their mother, he thought. Within him sadness settled like a heavy weight. He reached out and drew his daughter onto his knees.

"You do not remember your mother, do you?" he asked sadly. He stroked Hiki-mauna-lei's hair where it fell down her back like the cascade of Nā-molokama.

The children shook their heads. They could not remember.

"I look into your faces," he said, "and I see her again. I wish she were here to help you. Until now, you have been content to do as you were told. But now your thoughts fly to those children who play in Kalalau in the sunlight. But we Mū are an ancient people, born of Lua-mu'u in the time of pō, the deep night. Like our cousins, the Menehune, we cannot go into the sunshine. We must never allow a ray of sunshine to touch us. If it does, we will be turned to stone."

"Then that is why we cannot play with the children," Ku-a said.

"It is why you cannot go into the sun," Nā-'iwi corrected. "It has nothing to do with the children."

"So we would be turned to stone if we are touched by the sun," murmured Hiki. "Is that what happened to our mother?"

Nā-'iwi replied softly, "Your mother heard the women below beating out their tapa and talking and laughing together. 'I am tired of being alone,' she told me. 'I long to be friends with these women I can hear.' Nothing I could say helped her to forget this desire of hers." He stopped for, as he remembered, grief sat on his tongue and weighed it down so it could barely move.

"Then what happened?" demanded Hiki.

"One day," Nā-'iwi continued, "she could bear it no longer. 'I do not believe it,' she cried. 'Nobody turns to stone. People die and their bones are left. Bones, not stone! I am going down to Kalalau!' She walked out of the cave, out of the forest, into a meadow of grass and fern. There the sunlight fell upon her. She turned to stone before my eyes."

For a time, there was no sound in the cave. Then a breeze rattled the mat across the cave opening and the faint sound of someone calling to another down on the floor of Kalalau echoed along the cliffs.

"We will not go into the sunshine," Ku-a promised. "Will we, Hiki-mauna-lei?"

His sister shook her head. "We shall sleep in the day and play only at night," she said and yawned. "I am sleepy now."

"Come, sleep then," said Nā-'iwi. The children stretched out on their fragrant beds of fern and their father covered them with a thin, soft cover of woven banana leaves. They fell asleep, but Nā-'iwi remained beside the fire, remembering.

When the last ray of sunshine lifted from the ridges, Nā-'iwi woke his children. "I must tend to the bananas," he said. "Take as many bananas as you can carry down to the village and trade them for other food." In this way they had often bartered for food from the sea. The shore was not safe at night. The long swells could not be seen until too late.

Nā-'iwi set out in the darkness, but his large eyes were used to the starlight and he could see like an owl. There was much to do, for there were no seasons here in the uplands, and banana could be planted and harvested throughout the year. So each night, Nā-'iwi would find a place and dig a deep, wide hole. Then he would go to a banana tree and select a huli growing under a hanging bunch of fruit. This sucker would grow to bear fruit, for it had seen what it must do. Then Nā-'iwi sat down and ate until his stomach was full before he planted the huli, for if a farmer planted when his stomach was empty and thin, the bananas would become thin and sour, too. Next Nā-'iwi put the huli on his back and, bent over and staggering as though he were carrying a tremendous weight, went to plant the huli in the hole he had dug. Then he cultivated all his trees. When a bunch was ready, he would cut it down and place it in a large calabash where the fruit would ripen. Throughout his nights, Nā-'iwi was sad, for everything reminded him of his losses: the sad song of the 'i-'iwi for whom he had been named, the heaviness of the huli which was like the heaviness of his sorrow, the banana plants themselves whose fruit hung like golden frozen tears.

Meanwhile, Ku-a and Hiki bundled up hands of bananas and carefully climbed down the ridge until they reached the village. The village women were glad to see them, for these wild, bushy-haired children always brought the pink-fleshed bananas that were not forbidden to women. Men might eat any banana, but women were allowed only to eat the iholena, the pōpōʻulu and the kaualau. So the children had no trouble trading their fruit for some red seaweed and mū, a fish the women saved especially for them since it carried the same name as the wild people. Ku-a and Hiki left the village as silently as they had stayed in it, but once they were beyond the light of the fire, turned to look at the houses.

"The children are sleeping in there," Hiki whispered to her brother. "I wish I could play with them."

"They only sleep at night," Ku-a whispered back. "They play during the day when we must sleep. Come, we must go back."

She shook off his hand. "I want to at least see them," she said. "Let me at least watch them while they sleep."

The two children of Nā-ʻiwi crept up to a doorway and peered in where many children slept. Hiki stared for a long time. Tears filled her eyes as she turned away from the doorway. Silently the brother and sister began the long, steep climb to their home.

On their way, they picked the ʻākala berries, the wild raspberries that grew everywhere and gave its name to the valley. As they stopped to rest, Hiki said, "Couldn't we make some kind of cover that would keep the sunlight from touching us as we played with those children?"

"What could we make that would keep all the rays of sun from us?" Ku-a demanded. "No hat could have a brim large enough to shade us. But even if we could make such hats, who would play with us? We would look funny."

"I suppose so," admitted Hiki. She burst into tears. "But it is easy for you. You do not want to play with the children as much as I do."

"I do so," Ku-a said indignantly. "There are boys of my age living in Kalalau. They have bows and arrows to shoot at rats. I have made a bow, too, but I cannot use it at night. I cannot watch the flight of my arrow." For a moment his blood surged strongly through his body. He could beat anyone at hunting rats with bow and arrow. He knew he could. Then Ku-a remembered. In a flat, hopeless voice, he went on. "But since we can never play with the Kalalau children, we must try to forget them."

They could not forget, however. As they lay on their beds, the sound of children's laughter reached them. On the dark nights when they traded their bananas for fish, they would creep to the doorway and stare at the sleeping children. There was nothing they could do, nothing they could make that would help them.

But one night, the moon shone brilliantly in the sky, lighting all the leaves of the forest and all the pebbles in the path. "It will be easy to climb the trail tonight," Ku-a said happily. The children gathered up some hands of bananas and swiftly sped down the path into Kalalau.

They neared the village. They heard a burst of laughter coming from the grassy clearing just ahead. Startled, the children of Nā-'iwi stood at the clearing's edge and stared with wonder. The Kalalau children were playing in the moonlight. Their shouts of laughter awakened the birds nesting on the cliffs. With greedy eyes, Ku-a and Hiki watched the games until their arms grew weary from holding the bundles of bananas.

Putting down the burden, Hiki reached out to touch her brother. "Ku-a," she whispered, "the children are playing in the moonlight!" Even in her wildest schemes Hiki had never thought of this and happiness filled her with such lightness that her feet began to dance.

"Ku-a!" she called, "this is moonlight! We can play with them!"

She danced out of the trees' shadow and into the clearing, pulling Ku-a with her. They came close to the playing youngsters and then stopped, shy and embarrassed.

With noisy welcoming shouts, the Kalalau children surrounded Ku-a and Hiki. Then all were off in a swift game of tag. All the longings of Ku-a and Hiki were forgotten in this breathless swift game. The moon sailed along her charted course as the hours sped by.

Hiki at last played pahipahi. Her hands slapped the palms of another girl in intricate rhythms and designs of seven, as the other girls, circling them, chanted an accompaniment.

Ku-a played pana'iole with the boys. While some scooped out a steep-sided hole, others caught rats. With arrows of cane tassels, the boys shot at the rats as they scurried and dodged in the trap. Ku-a was too excited to be finally playing to keep a steady hand. But that did not matter!

In the night winds, the children flew kites, the round kites, the winged kites, and the crescent kites, honoring the moon that lit their play. The hours fled past, unmarked and unnoticed.

Hiki fell to the ground, breathless with laughter. She was facing the steep cliffs. Her eyes widened in surprise. She leapt to her feet, the laughter gone. "Ku-a!" she called. "Look! The east is red! The sun is coming!"

Swiftly the children of Nā'iwi ran up the trail toward their cave home so far above them. Fear bit at their legs like angry dogs. They climbed desperately, using any hold their hands and feet could find.

"Ku-a, wait!" cried Hiki. "I am out of breath!"

"Hurry, hurry!" Ku-a urged. We must get home before the sun comes!"

On and on they struggled. Ku-a turned to reach out for his sister's hand. In that moment, the sun rose from his resting place and stretched mightily. A finger of sunlight flew out to touch the children.

"Ku-a!" Hiki cried out and was still.

"My sister!" Ku-a cried out and was still.

Nā'iwi was waiting for his children to return home. When the sun had risen and they had not come, Nā'iwi was filled with dread. He tried to reassure himself that they had found shelter from the day, but he did not really believe it. He left the cave and searched the shadowy woods, calling their names. They did not answer.

He came to the edge of the forest and looked down the steep path to Kalalau. There on the steepest part of the razorbacked ridge, he saw two large stones that had not been there before. Tears filled his eyes.

"Now I am alone," he wept. "Oh, my children!"

He stayed at the edge of the forest through the long day, and when night finally came he walked down to the stones that are the children of Nā'iwi. He sat beside them in silent sorrow through most of the night.

At last he rose. He gently touched the stone that had been Ku-a-pōhaku. He stroked the stone that had been Hiki-mauna-lei. Then without looking back he walked swiftly up the path, past his cave, past his banana trees until he came to an open meadow. There, near the center, was a large stone. The sun was rising and the i'iwi birds darted among the lehua blossoms to suck the nectar.

Nā'iwi stood facing the rock as the first rays of sun fell into the clearing. "Our children are gone," he said. "Oh, my wife, I am lonely."

Nā'iwi wept and the heavy weight of his grief melted away. With a light step, he walked out to stand beside his wife in the bright sunshine.

KE-AHI-LELE O KA-MAILE

In the days when the great double canoes still traveled the ocean between Kahiki and Hawai'i, a high chiefess named Ka-maile ruled over Nu'alolo valley. Even on an island always famous for the beauty of its women, she was considered beautiful. She was tall and moved with the grace and strength of a trained athlete or a dancer. Her hair had hints of firelight in it. The tapa she wore had a few leaves of maile pounded into it and she always wore a garland of the fragrant vine, so that she seemed to walk in a cloud of fragrance.

Her compound of houses was high on the ridge overlooking the valley, beside the trail that led upwards into Kōke'e. From the compound, the trail descended steeply along the ridge to a place called Alapi'i. Here, where the cliff fell back under itself, four rings had been carved from the rock and a rope ladder had been attached to them. The traveler had to swing down the ladder with his feet dangling over the roaring ocean before reaching a narrow trail that continued down to the beach. Only those born and raised in Nu'alolo, or those who were fearless, made this journey with ease.

From her compound, Ka-maile could look down into Nu'alolo, down on the taro patches, the houses nestled against the cliffs, the groves of kukui trees, down onto the grassy sand dunes, and over the sea that stretched blue and gray to the horizon. The ocean was very deep here and the protective reef very small. Yet the people lived here pleasantly enough, growing food for their own needs and raising pigs. The hair of these pigs was pure black. There was no other color on them. Because of this, whenever a large canoe was built anywhere on the island, the priests and chiefs concerned would travel to Nu'alolo to obtain one of these pigs that they would sacrifice to the gods. Then the pig would be cooked and eaten in a special ceremony to insure the sturdiness and safety of the canoe. These black pigs and their place in the canoe-builders ceremony gave Nu'alolo its name.

Whenever the priests and chiefs came, Ka-maile would order a special bonfire lit at the top of the cliff near her home. Into this fire, specially wrapped branches of hau would be placed so that the soft inner core would catch on fire. Then the branch would be twirled around a thrower's head and flung out over the cliff edge. The wind, blowing from Kōke'e, would catch the firebrand and swirl it around the skies until it fell hissing into the ocean. As the brand soared, embers and flames marked its path, creating a spectacle that remained fixed in the memory of the spectators. The leaping fires of Ka-maile were as famous as the black sacrificial pigs of Nu'alolo.

Of course, all the unmarried chiefs who came attempted to win Ka-maile as a wife. Her gentle answer was always the same: "I have not yet found the man who will take my heart." No suitor left her in anger. Each had seen Ka-maile's beauty, smelled the fragrance of her maile, heard the softness of her voice. And, too, each had noticed the young steward who was her constant companion and wondered how long it would be before the chiefess would notice his devotion to her.

The people of Nu'alolo named the young steward Kūpono-aloha, because it was so obvious to them that he loved Ka-maile. Kūpono-aloha had loved her for as long as he could remember. He had watched her beauty unfold like a flower bud. Whenever she had walked along the cliff edge of Nā-pali, he had been with her. They had looked down into Hanakāpī'ai valley and he had told her the story of the dwarf fish that live there. He had told her the story of the Nā'iwi children. He had become her steward, for his rank was as high as hers, an invaluable extra right hand that settled disputes quickly and peacefully, that enforced water rights to all the taro terraces, that tended to all the details that affect a community's well-being.

He had loved her for a long time and at last one night as they watched the firebrands sailing through the skies, he said, "Ka-maile, you know how much I love you. Will you be my wife?"

She touched his arm gently. "I know the people call you Kūpono-aloha," she teased, "because you go around sighing about love. But we have known each other since I was born. We are like brother and sister. I love you as I would a brother, but nothing more."

"My love is greater than that of a brother for a sister," Kūpono-aloha protested.

"You blind yourself with thoughts of love," she said. "Look around the island of Kauai. It is full of lovely women. Search this island for a woman who will capture and hold your heart."

"I have seen the beauties of Kauai," he replied. "It is you who have captured and hold my heart."

"That is too bad," she replied. "I am fond of you, but I do not want to be your wife. Love is like one of those firebrands we are watching. No one can make it follow a chosen path. It floats free and no one can catch it as it flies. And even if you did catch it, the fire would have gone out and you would hold only an empty burnt stick."

"And if I could catch it while it still burns," he said hopefully, "would you then believe me and consider me as a husband?"

"No one can catch one of those firesticks," Ka-maile replied. "Too many people have been hurt trying it. It cannot be done."

"Yet I will try it," Kūpono-aloha said.

He went swiftly down the trail and reached the sand dunes. He watched the flight patterns of the soaring firebrands, searching for one that might fall near his reach. "Oh, gods," he prayed, "you know of my love for Ka-maile. Help me reach her heart. Help me catch a firebrand."

The gods heard him and sent the wind named 'Aiko'o, the wind that eats canoes. It was a strong wind and blew up huge waves to crash on the beach. 'Aiko'o blew the firebrands easterly around Mākuaiki point. Kūpono-aloha clambered over the rocks and swam the dangerous waves to reach the little beach formed by Ka-āhole stream. As he came ashore, the wind stopped for a moment and a firebrand fell into his waiting hands. Then 'Aiko'o blew hard again. There would be no returning to Nu'alolo against the wind, so Kūpono-aloha found a sheltered spot and lay down to sleep.

In the morning, Kūpono-aloha climbed the steep ravine of Ka-āhole and arrived, bruised and scratched, at Ka-maile's compound, holding the firebrand he had caught. The compound was empty of people. From the beach Kūpono-aloha heard people shouting. Out at sea, red sails filled with wind drove a double canoe through the heavy swells. It was a large canoe used for travel between the islands, big enough even for the voyage to Kahiki. Kūpono-aloha saw a man carrying a bowl step to the front of the canoe. He knocked the bowl against the hull several times. A fin cut through the water and a huge shark surfaced beside the man. The shark opened its jaws and the man poured the contents of the bowl into it. Then the shark sank down out of sight and the canoe raced on for the shore.

Kūpono-aloha, anxious to show the firebrand to Ka-maile, hurried down the trail and reached the beach just as the hundred-foot-long canoe hissed onto the sand. The forty rowers raised their paddles with a shout. A man wearing the insignia of a chief jumped down and strode to the waiting Ka-maile.

"Welcome, chief," Ka-maile greeted him. "Welcome to Nu'alolo."

"Sweet welcome, indeed," the chief answered. "I am 'Ō'ili-ku-ka-heana of Kahiki. We have been sailing for a long time seeking a hospitable place where we can plant the 'awa cuttings we have brought."

"Search the valley and ridges of Nu'alolo," Ka-maile invited. "If you find a place suitable for your planting, it shall be yours. I offer you the hospitality of Nu'alolo. Kūpono-aloha, show them to the visitors' compound."

The Kahiki chief looked at the steward and smiled in amusement. "Your steward is bruised and bloody from scratches," he said, "and carries a strange stick snatched from the fire. What custom is this?"

"This is a firebrand," Kūpono-aloha replied. "I caught it last night and the bruises and scratches are from my attempt. There is no custom."

"A firebrand?" laughed the Kahiki chief. "Is it like this?" he asked, snapping his fingers at one of his men and pointing down the beach. The servant ran, picked up a stick from the ocean's edge and brought it to his chief. "Now I have one, too," the chief said. "Anyone can catch a firebrand such as this."

"I caught this one as it flew, blazing with embers," Kūpono-aloha replied.

"What proof do you have?" asked 'Ō'ili-ku-ka-heana. "Did anyone see you? How can anyone tell you caught fire from the sky and did not find one washed up on the beach?" The Kahiki chief asked these questions in an earnest way as though he truly wanted the answers. Kūpono-aloha could not answer. He was saved from embarrassment when Ka-maile spoke to him.

"Show our guests to their compound," she ordered. "See that food is brought to them. Tonight we will feast and display the soaring fires of Nu'alolo."

That night the firebrands flew again. They sailed far up into the sky, looking down on Kāmaulele where lava still boiled. They sailed far out to sea, disturbing the birds nesting on Ka'ula island. Standing alone on the beach, Kūpono-aloha waited for a firebrand to fall towards him, and when one did, he caught it. The center of the branch still burned and the end was hot. As he held this fire, Kūpono-aloha thought, "What can I do to prove my love for Ka-maile?" He paused for a moment, then pressed the burning edge against his chest, branding himself with the leaping fire of Nu'alolo.

He climbed to the compound of Ka-maile. The Kahiki chief and the Nuʻalolo chiefess were sitting where they could watch the firebrand display. Ka-maile turned to her steward with shining eyes and exclaimed, "Kūpono-aloha, rejoice with me. I have found the man who has won my heart. ʻŌ-ili-ku-ka-heana has asked me to marry him and I have consented. Together we will raise this ʻawa plant he has brought with him. Be happy for me!"

Ka-maile never noticed the blistered ring of flesh on her steward's chest. She never noticed when the blisters faded and a ring of scar tissue formed. Ka-maile was too busy. The plant that ʻŌ-ili-ku-ka-heana had brought was a demanding one. There was much work and the Kahiki chief insisted that only she could do most of it. It was a special plant, he told her, and these first cuttings must be tended with great care, for if they died, they could not be replaced.

First of all, the cuttings her husband had brought with him were placed in a trench and covered with a mulch of leaves. When they had sprouted, each cutting was placed in a hill of heaped-up dirt and rotting leaves. For three years the plants grew, watched over, weeded, watered by Ka-maile's own labor. The plants grew taller than the chiefess. The leaves were heart-shaped and grew on short yellow-ish-green stems. The large bush gave off a smell like the mokihana berries found in the forests of Kōkeʻe.

Now ʻŌ-ili-ku-ka-heana showed Ka-maile the proper way to make use of this plant. He first bathed in the ocean, then in the fresh water of a stream, to cleanse himself. After rinsing his mouth with water containing olonā and putting on a clean malo, he cut the plant just above the ground level. He grasped the stump and tore the root from the ground. Rising to his feet, he lifted the root toward the sky. Then he handed the root to Ka-maile. The plant itself was cut into pieces and planted in a trench to begin a new cycle of growth.

Ka-maile took the root, washed it, and scraped off the hair-like rootlets. When it was dry, she pounded the root into small pieces. Rinsing her mouth with a mixture of wood ash and water, she picked up a small piece, placed it in her mouth, and chewed. When the ʻawa root was completely chewed into a pulp, she spit the mouthful into a bowl and began again with more root.

After the root had been thoroughly chewed, which took several days, fresh water was added to the bowl and the mixture was carefully strained.

Now the 'awa was ready to drink.

It was a bitter drink, and bananas and sugar cane were always on hand to sweeten the mouth. What it did to the drinker was worth the taste. It was intoxicating. The world looked different and the drinker felt as though some new secret world was opening to him as he left behind this world. Colors were brighter, the wind's caress softer, the voice of the waterfall clearer. It was a magical place reached only by drinking 'awa.

By day, Ka-maile worked hard in the grove of 'awa plants, chewing, chewing, chewing the bitter root. By night she and her husband drank the 'awa and reached the magical land opened to them. Ka-maile was too busy with 'awa to attend to anything else and the duties she had in Nu'alolo fell to her steward.

Ka-maile learned that when her ears rang, like strong winds roaring or like the whistlings of land shells, she must lie perfectly still to avoid being sick. The lure of the 'awa was too strong to let this discomfort stop her. As the nights passed to weeks, the weeks to months, her skin became covered with white scales. Her eyes grew red and inflamed. Her arms and legs became thin and her whole body trembled and shook. She found it hard to raise her head. She cared for nothing but the comfort she found in drinking 'awa.

Over the years, the 'awa bushes flourished. There was a grove of the mokihana-scented shrub stretching around the compound of the Nu'alolo chiefess. The cuttings brought by 'Ō'ili-ku-ka-heana from Kahiki had established the plant on this island and there was now a group of people addicted to the bitter drink. 'Ō'ili-ku-ka-heana was satisfied. He looked at the woman he had married. Her beauty was gone, her face a mask of white scales and inflamed eyes.

"Now you know the pleasure of 'awa," he told Kamaile. "There is no need for me to remain here. I shall continue my journey."

'Ō'ili-ku-ka-heana called his paddlers together. They collected cuttings of 'awa to take to new places. They launched the huge canoe, paddled beyond the breakers, and held the canoe steady. 'Ō'ili-ku-ka-heana banged a bowl of 'awa against the hull and a large, gray shark emerged from the depths. 'Ō'ili-ku-ka-heana poured the bitter drink into the shark's open mouth. The shark then swam lazily toward the west, picking up speed as the red sail was raised to catch the wind and the paddlers dipped their oars into the ocean, following the shark to a new landfall. Kamaile stood on the cliff and watched the canoe, led by its shark guide, disappear into the horizon. She returned to her sleeping house and poured some water into a wooden bowl. She placed a flat stone into the water and, as the ripples died away on the bowl's rim, she stared at her reflection.

After a long time she laughed bitterly. "I have been a fool," she said. Anger filled her shaking body. "'Awa is a poison."

She staggered angrily from the compound and went to the grove of 'awa. One by one she cut down every plant. As she attempted to pull the first of the roots from the ground, her strength failed her and she sat loose-limbed in despair. In that moment, Kūpono-aloha kneeled beside her and pulled the root free from the ground.

"All!" she urged him. "Pull all the roots up!"

Kūpono-aloha obeyed her. Before the sun set, the 'awa plants were tied into a bundle. Kamaile, in a blaze of strength, threw the 'awa away.

Caught by the winds, the 'awa bundle fell on the slopes of Kawaikini where it grew, forgotten by all, until at a later time and in another story it was found again.

Kūpono-aloha helped Kamaile and the others who had indulged in the bitter drink regain their strength. He interested her once again in the comings and goings of the Nu'alolo people and of the visitors who came for the black pigs. The effects of the 'awa faded. Her eyes cleared, she could hold up her head, her legs and arms fleshed out, her skin became soft and golden again.

One evening the soaring fires of Nu'alolo flew out over the steep-sided valley. The chiefess and her steward sat together in companionable silence. She turned to say something to him and her eye was caught by a sudden flicker of light from the bonfire falling on the circular scar on Kūpono-aloha's chest. In that moment she understood what he had done and what it meant.

"You caught a firebrand," she murmured, reaching out to touch the scar.

"Yes."

What more was there to say? Kūpono-aloha's strong love won him Kamaile as his wife. Together they ruled over Nu'alolo. The leaping fire of Kamaile brought many chiefs wishing to prove the depths of their love by catching firebrands from the sky and pressing them on themselves to make the scar of Kūpono-aloha.

NOU O MAKANA

CHRISTINE FAYE

NOU O MAKANA

When the Menehune still lived on Kauai, a high chief of Hale-le'a and his followers came to visit the sandy plains of Hā'ena. He came to catch a firebrand from the fireworks cliff of Makana to prove his affection for a woman who did not believe he loved her. If he could catch a firebrand before it fell into the sea, his love would be unquestioned. And if he could catch that one brand that flew the farthest out he would prove his feelings beyond all doubt.

So Kahua-nui, high chiefess of Hā'ena, ordered the firethrowers to wrap dry branches of hau in twine made of the silver-gray hinahina. These they would carry on their backs up the Limahuli valley and climb the steep slopes to the top of Makana. There, standing at the edge of the thousand-foot cliff, they would set the brands on fire and throw them out over the edge. These small logs, caught by the wind currents, would swirl out over the land into the sea, leaving a trail of glowing embers as they rose and fell like sea birds soaring in the wind.

Nou had always wanted to go to the top of the cliff, to Makana, with the firethrowers. His dark eyes had often watched the firebrands sailing across the dark skies of night and in his heart the dream of being a firethrower burned as brightly as the embers themselves.

"Let me go with you," he begged the busy firethrowers. "Please let me go with you."

"You are still too young," the leader of the firethrowers said. "Stay here and practice throwing twigs until your arms grow strong and your wrists supple. This is no boy's play we go to do." The leader's thoughts turned to the rich gifts the chief of Hale-le'a had promised to the man whose brand he caught that night. So each firethrower was intent on tying a knot different from any other man's and his thoughts were not upon the hopes of a youngster.

The men picked up their bundles of wrapped hau and set out to climb the steep trail. Nou watched them go. But this time he was not content to remain and watch from the beach. He began to follow the men up the steep path to the top. Once there, he hoped, perhaps they would let him throw one log, even a little one. At least then part of his dream would come true. He wanted to tell his friends, "I threw a log from Makana and it went far out to sea, farther than anyone else's! I did that!" But how could he get to throw anything over the cliff if the firethrowers would not let him go with them? So Nou followed without permission and climbed the steep trail.

Nou struggled up the path and soon his breath came in painful gasps. He could not step from toehold to toehold as the men did for his boy's legs were too short. He had to climb over and around rocks and boulders, grasping handfuls of the coarse grass to keep from falling over the steep cliffs. At last he was forced to rest.

As he sat, Nou heard someone calling over the wind that hummed about his ears.

"Help me!" the voice called. "I am caught and cannot get free!"

Nou looked around. He could see no one.

"Help me!" the voice groaned.

Guided by the broken call of the strange voice, Nou found the caller, a tiny man, hardly taller than Nou, with a long, brown beard and friendly eyes. A large rock had rolled across the little man's legs. He was caught on the edge of a steep drop and could not free himself without falling.

"Help me!" called the little man once again. "Come, I will not hurt you."

Nou approached, undecided whether to help the man or run away. "What can I do?" he asked doubtfully.

"Push at this rock," the little man said, "as I hold onto the grass."

Nou did as he was asked and shoved against the large rock. It tipped and fell over the cliff and the man was free.

The little man stood up on his uncertain legs and thanked Nou. "I am a Menehune," he said. "Tell me one thing that you wish for and I will do it in thanks for what you have done for me." The Menehune shuddered and said, "The morning sun would have turned me to stone. Please tell me what I can do for you."

Nou thought for only a moment. "This is my dream," he said. "I want to throw at least one log from Makana, even a little one, so I can say I threw a firebrand and it went far out to sea, farther than anyone else has ever thrown it. This is what I wish."

"It is a little thing," the Menehune said. "I can help you to throw those logs so that you will always be the best thrower. You shall do this tonight. But you must do as I tell you." The Menehune whispered in Nou's ear so softly that not even the birds that flew low over them could hear what was said. "Follow closely what I have told you," finished the Menehune, "and your dream shall come true."

Nou continued to climb the rest of the way to the top of Makana. As the Menehune had told him, the firethrowers were very angry with him.

"Go home," they ordered. "This is no place for you. Even if it were, you brought no firebrands with you. Here one throws only what one brings."

Nou stepped forward and spoke to the men preparing the fire. "Let me stay," he said quietly but firmly. "I will make a bet with you. I will give my life against anything you care to wager that I can throw a firebrand farther out to sea than any of you."

"You have nothing I want," one firethrower said.

"Take care," growled another. "It is a dangerous thing you say."

"The chief of Hale-le'a has offered a prize to the man whose brand he catches," another man said. "We do not have time for a boy's silly game."

"I will take only one of the brands and I will win my life back," Nou said. "Will you let me throw?"

"So be it," said the leader of the firethrowers. "If you are stupid enough to make such a bet, you who have never done this before against we who are experienced, and wish to lose your life, I shall not stop you. I will even give you one of my firebrands."

The men ignored Nou and silently prepared for the fireworks display of Makana. The hau logs, tightly wrapped in hinahina, were put into the bonfire so that the soft centers would burn. Nou untied the end of the hinahina rope on the brand the leader gave him, and retied it in the special knot the Menehune had taught him.

Then, on top of Makana, it was time. The first man threw his log. All his skill, all his experience guided the fiery brand. It went far out over the ocean, sparks marking a trail against the night. Another and another man threw. Never had the people below seen such a spectacle as log after log soared, now low, now high, and flew far from shore to drop at last into the sea.

Then the leader of the firethrowers threw and the log went far, far out to sea. It was against such a throw that Nou must do his best.

Finally, the men stepped back and motioned to Nou to throw. The boy picked up his firebrand. It was unexpectedly heavy and hot to his touch. "Help me!" he whispered. "If I lose, I will die."

He remembered the words of the Menehune. "This is the only way you will be allowed to throw. Trust me. I shall not let you die."

Nou grasped the smoldering log firmly in his hands. It was as tall as himself and the glowing embers sparked fiercely. He lifted it, feeling for the point of balance. He began twirling it over his head, slowly at first, then faster and faster. He spun on his heels and with a great heave let go of the brand.

It flew across the clearing and dropped out of sight, falling straight down the face of the cliff. Embers touched the rocks, which flashed with reflections like shiny eyes opened wide in surprise.

The men laughed. "The braggart dies," they exclaimed. "His log falls straight to the bottom of Makana." They caught Nou by his legs and arms, making ready for a final throw that night.

In that moment, the wind came from the mountains, chilling the shoulders of the firethrowers and stopping their motion. The wind flowed down the cliff face and caught Nou's brand like a child grasps a new toy. Amused and playful, the wind toyed with the brand, tossing it now this way, now that way, throwing it far into the sky and letting it drop nearly to the ground before catching it and flinging it high again. Slowly wind and firebrand played above the sand dunes of Hā'ena, over the reef, and over the sea. The brand, its embers tracing its path through the sky, drifted slowly, gliding on the wind's breath. It hovered above the heads of the spectators, looped over and over, soared, a child's plaything. The wind carried the brand far out to sea and, tired of the game, dropped its toy into the waiting hand of the chief of Hale-le'a.

The firethrowers watched in growing amazement, for Nou's firebrand had indeed flown far, so far he might have won his bet. They set the boy on his feet. The leader kicked the bonfire over the edge of Makana to signal those below that the firebrands had all flown. Then they settled down to sleep.

The next morning the firethrowers eagerly gathered before their chiefess Kahua-nui and her guest, the chief of Hale-le'a. The firebrand that had flown the farthest was in the chief's hand. He handed it to the firethrower's leader.

"Whose firebrand is this?" the chief asked. "Whose hand threw it? Let him come forward."

The leader looked at the end knots of the hinahina wrapping. His face grew dark. "It is Nou's firebrand," he said.

The youngster stepped forward and kneeled before the chief.

"Come, don't joke with me," laughed the chief. "This boy couldn't make a throw like that."

The firethrowers, angry as they were at the boy, still told the truth. They told the chief of the bet and at last the chief understood that this was no joke, that this boy had indeed made the winning throw.

"I can't believe it," the chief said. "That such a youngster could make a throw like that! Let's see if indeed it was so. Tonight," he said to Nou, "you will throw again, throw and throw until you equal the mark you set last night. You will go up with only my trusted bodyguards to act as my witnesses. I shall be waiting in my canoe for your brands to fall. Then and only then will I believe. If you fail, you will die."

Nou gathered whatever branches of hau he could find drying on the shore, for none of the firethrowers offered to help him. Nou gathered fresh hinahina from the beach, too fresh, too green to burn, but he wrapped the vines around the hau for he had nothing else. Although he knew he might die tomorrow, his heart sang. He had indeed had his heart's desire. He had thrown a firebrand and it had soared farther than any other. He took the time to catch freshwater shrimp from the stream of Limahuli, for shrimp are the favorite food of Menehune. Nou could think of no better way to thank the small man for his help.

When there was barely enough time to make the steep climb to Makana, Nou bundled up his firebrands and his parcel of shrimp and set out. The chief's men followed him closely, but offered no help.

When they reached the top of Makana, Nou lit a bonfire. Just as twilight came, the boy said to the bodyguards, "Let me go apart and make my prayers."

Out of sound of the guards, Nou called softly to the Menehune. "Come," he whispered, "I need you now."

The Menehune stepped out from behind a rock. Nou handed him the bundle of shrimp. "Thank you for last night," he said.

"There was no need for this, but I thank you," the Menehune said. "I know why you are here tonight. We will play together. Have no fear. Go throw your brands."

Nou returned to his fire. The darkness of night hid the chief's bodyguards. Nou looked down and saw the twinkling torches where hundreds of people watched, drawn by the news they had heard. He saw the torch on the canoe where the chief of Hale-le'a waited, out beyond the breakers. Nou reached for a firebrand, twirled it around his head, and threw it. The playful wind caught it and played with it as though it were a favorite toy. The embers flowing from the log marked the graceful arch of the flight.

Time and time again Nou threw his brands. The wind never tired of playing with these glowing toys. Each time the brand was carried to the waiting chief, but the mischievous wind would snatch the brand from the chief's grasp and plunge it into the ocean. Finally the last brand was thrown. Nou kicked the fire off the edge of the cliff and, caught in the wonder of what he had done, fell asleep.

The chief, of course, had to believe the word of his bodyguards. No one knew of the help that Nou had received from the Menehune. Even Nou did not know what help the Menehune had given him. He only knew that help had come.

The chief heaped honor upon honor on Nou. "You shall have the privileges of royalty," the chief proclaimed, "if you continue to make these magnificent throws. Surely in years to come the famous firebrands of Nou will be remembered!"

"These other men," the chief said scornfully, pointing to the firethrowers, "are but infants against the strength and skill of this child."

The firethrowers heard. There was no pleasure for them in Nou's triumph. In their hearts, there was only anger that a boy had done better than any of them.

"Take what I have been given," Nou pleaded with them. "I don't want these things." He thought they were angry with him because of the gifts he had been given.

The firethrowers refused to take any of the chief's gifts to Nou. Together they plotted to rid themselves of this boy who had made fools of them all.

They invited Nou to go with them once again to Makana to throw the firebrands. Nou went with them happily, carrying a bundle of freshwater shrimp in his hand. Near the top, just before the last steep climb when a man must go hand over hand, the men caught Nou and quickly took the life from his body. The boy was stuffed into a small cave alongside the path. Then the men continued on their way.

Once they were gone, the Menehune came out from his hiding place and stood beside the cave where Nou lay silently, the bundle of shrimp still clutched in his hand. With tears streaming down his cheeks, the Menehune spoke.

"Nou, my little friend, I am powerless to keep this death from you. I have not helped you as you helped me. But this I promise. I will keep the firethrowers from disturbing you again and let you rest in peace. Farewell, my friend."

Early the next morning, the firethrowers returned to fling Nou's body over the edge of the cliff. But they could not, because within the cave's entrance, filling it from side to side, was a Menehune. The little man of flesh and blood was already turning into hard stone. Only the Menehune's head was still free. He spoke to the fearful men. "Go! you men who have murdered, for you may not touch Nou's body again. I turn myself to stone to guard him. Go! May your bones ache and your footsteps be painful forever!"

With this curse, the Menehune was gone. Only stone remained, forever guarding the burial place of his friend, Nou, famous firethrower of Makana at Hā'ena.

The firebrand throwers returned to the beach and could only say that Nou had fallen on the way up and they had not been able to recover his body. But after that they never climbed Makana again, for their bones ached and they could not walk without pain.

Even today the Menehune who turned himself to stone remains guarding the grave of his friend Nou. No one ever found out how the Menehune had helped Nou. Some said the Menehune had power over the winds. Others say he blew from his puckered mouth and it was his breath that carried the firebrands of Nou far out over the ocean.

But who knows? Who can tell?

The Menehune were leaving their homes on Kauai. For many years they had lived on this island, these small, strong people who worked only at night. When they first came, only the Mū lived on the land. The Mū were small, too, and few of number and lived in the deep valleys. Then tall strangers from Kahiki arrived and settled. For a time the two groups lived apart, the Menehune working at night, the Hawaiians by day.

After they had been living side by side for some time, the Menehune king found that many of his men were marrying Hawaiian women. These men began to teach their children the Menehune way of doing things, but their Hawaiian mothers also taught them the Hawaiian ways. The Menehune king grew worried because the two groups were mingling, and he feared his smaller people would be swallowed by the larger. At last, he decided to leave the island of Kauai with all his people.

He gathered the Menehune from all corners of the land and they met at Māhie in Kōkeʻe. They formed into ranks and began the march to Hāʻena where their canoes were waiting for them.

At the top of a steep and unnamed valley, the Menehune paused. Hanakāpīʻai, a favorite princess, gave birth to a child. Within a week, however, she died. The grief of the Menehune grew when Hanakoa, sister of Hanakāpīʻai, slipped on a stone and fell over the edge of a cliff into a small valley. These two valleys were named after the princesses.

The king of the Menehune ordered a period of mourning for these two women, so dearly loved by all. For sixty days, the Menehune would remain where they were as a mark of respect and sorrow.

Only one problem remained. The large numbers of persons had to be fed.

So the Menehune king called his head fisherman, Manini-holo, before him. "Chief fisherman," he said, "my people are hungry. Take your fishermen and go to Hāʻena and bring us fish to eat."

Manini-holo bowed before the king. "It shall be done," he said.

Manini-holo gathered his men together and they went on to Hāʻena. There Manini-holo formed the fishermen into groups. "Tonight," he told them, "we will gather fish and seafood from the reef."

He ordered the kukui torches lit. Then the groups spread out along the reef from Kēʻē point to Ka-ūmaka, along the shorelines of Hāʻena. One group dove from the reef to spear the fish swimming in the shallow ocean. Another group gathered wana, ʻopihi, loli, and limu from the reef itself. A group searched for the squid and the eel, luring them from their holes and catching them barehanded. Lobsters, too, were caught. Every rock was searched by busy fingers. Hand nets and gill nets were used, and baskets of seafood were brought to the sandy plain beside Mānoa stream where Manini-holo, from a place above the steep cliff, directed the activities.

The baskets were emptied on mats of ti leaves. The fish were cleaned and wrapped into bundles that could be carried back to hungry friends and relatives. When each man and woman had two bundles apiece to carry, Manini-holo ordered the rest of the fish to be properly stored so they could be found in good condition when the fishing crew returned again.

When the eastern horizon first paled from blackest night, Manini-holo called his men and women together. "The sun puts a stop to our work," he told them. "Here are the bundles of food we have caught this night. Each of you take two bundles. We return to our king."

The Menehune picked up the bundles and began the journey back up the steep trail to Kōkeʻe. Manini-holo checked the fish they had to leave behind them. It was a large pile, twenty times taller than the little man. The fish were covered with ti leaves and sprinkled with salt water. They were piled against the smooth face of the cliff beneath kukui trees where the cooling shade would keep them.

"These will remain fresh," Manini-holo said, "until we return in the evening to bring them to our king."

The Menehune ate well that day as they rested in places hidden from the sun. But hunger knows no rest and the fisherfolk went back to Hāʻena the next evening to collect the fish waiting there. But there were no fish neatly piled waiting for them. The fish were all gone. Only the ti leaves were left, scattered about the grassy plain beside Mānoa stream.

Manini-holo searched the area but could find no signs of whoever had stolen all the fish. He was a practical man and so did not waste time in idle wonderings. The Menehune must be fed. "There is nothing we can do to regain our lost fish," he told his fisherfolk. "We must catch more fish tonight to take to our people."

Making use of the scattered ti leaves, too sandy and old to be used for making bundles, Manini-holo ordered the leaves attached to a large net. This net was piled on the platform of a small double canoe. Manini-holo took his place on this canoe and, followed by two outrigger canoes, paddled far out to sea. Then he gave one end of the long net to the men of one canoe and the other end to the other canoe and ordered them to paddle ashore, making a wide arc as they brought the ends to shore. The net now was anchored at both ends to the shore where many people grasped the ends. The center was held by the double canoe to form a great semi-circle. The fish inside the net thought to swim away under the net, but the swaying ti leaves frightened them back toward the shore.

Manini-holo gave the signal and the people on shore pulled in the heavy net hand over hand. The men in the canoes beat the water with their paddles. When at last Manini-holo could step ashore from the double canoe, he stepped onto a beach piled high with fish. These were cleaned and wrapped into bundles. Once again a large pile of fish was left behind when the fisherfolk returned to the mountains that morning with their catch.

In the dim light of the next evening, Manini-holo and his fisherfolk returned to Hā'ena to find their large pile of fish had once again been stolen. This time the wind was still and the ti leaves lay as though someone had thrown them down.

"Let's search for this thief," Manini-holo said. His people carefully spread along the small plain, their sharp eyes peering carefully at the ground.

"The ti leaves are just tossed aside," said one of the Menehune.

"There are many footprints here in the sand," another Menehune exclaimed.

"Notice, too," said another, "that although there are footprints on the ti leaves, none of the leaves are torn. How can that be?"

"That means that the thief of our fish is an akua," said Manini-holo, "some sort of supernatural being, for only akua can walk on ti leaves without tearing them. We must search it out and destroy it, so he will not bother anyone again."

Manini-holo studied the pattern of footprints on the grassy plain, the marks on the ti leaves, the flattened grass. He followed the pattern of footprints to a small hole in the face of the cliff. There, deep in the rock, the akua slept the night away.

The chief fisherman called his people around him. "Listen to my plan," he said. "I will take half of you and we shall start digging into this cliff, chasing the akua before us. The others will move up the valley a little and dig into this cliff from the side. We will meet inside. Take your weapons for we must kill this mischievous being."

Half the Menehune fisherfolk went to the little hole and began digging. Quickly the rock was opened and they came across a small akua hiding in a cleft. Manini-holo speared the akua and it died. He looked carefully at it, a small being, something like a rat but larger. The fisherman shook his head. "There will be many of these," he said. "Continue digging."

The digging continued. The cave they were digging became large enough to hold them all and they dug out more and more rock as they followed the little akua into their hiding places. One by one the akua they found were put to death.

At last the two groups of fisherfolk met. "We have killed many akua," said the group that had come in from the side.

"So have we," said Manini-holo. "The work is done. We can fish now without thieves taking our catch away from us. Now there is little time left of this night. Catch what we can so we will not go back to our friends empty-handed."

The fisherfolk returned to the reef of Hāʻena and caught fish and eels and all the edible things that lived there. They carried home with them all they could put into the leaf bundles. They left behind them a small pile of fish, as a test to discover if more akua lived somewhere in the deep, tall cave they had dug that night.

When the Menehune returned the next evening, the pile of fish remained untouched beside the cave. The Menehune did not stay near the cave, however, for the bodies of the akua, filled as they were with the fish they had stolen, had begun to smell badly. For this reason the Menehune called the large cave they had dug Ka-hauna, the terrible smell, from the foul smell of the akua.

But, after the Menehune had left Kauai to be lost from the eyes of mankind forevermore, the smell of the bodies drifted away. When the smell had been forgotten, the people of Hāʻena wondered at the name of Ka-hauna.

They listened to the story of how this great cave came to be. In memory of the Menehune fisherman, they named the cave Manini-holo.

EPILOGUE

Here are eighteen stories of Kauai, gathered from many sources. Some of them were written down by W. H. Rice. Some of them are in Fornander, and in the writings of Hofgaard. One of them, Kawelo o Mānā, is found in a long footnote in Emerson's "Unwritten Literature of Hawaii." Some of them were told to me by Jacob Maka of Hāʻena. All of them tell stories of the earliest period of time in Kauai's history.

These stories have been lost except to those who enjoy digging in libraries. They have been gathered and retold to keep them from being forgotten. They have been designed to amuse the reader and will benefit from being read aloud. They are also intended to illustrate certain aspects of the ancient cultures and societies that flourished on this island.

One of the stories, Pōhaku-o-Kāne, is set in the period before settlement. Some of the stories tell of the Menehune and Mū peoples who lived here before the Hawaiians came. The others tell of people and events of the earliest Hawaiians. Like all folk stories, these cannot be proved to depict actual people, and, in fact, seem aimed at helping people remember certain places by name.

It is possible, using these stories, to generally reconstruct where the ancient roads and trails went. In order to get to Kōkeʻe from Hanalei, for instance, it was necessary to go up Wainiha valley to Maunahina before climbing to Kilohana, a trail that was used by Army engineers during World War II. In order to climb down into Kalalau from Kōkeʻe, it was helpful to know the rocks of the Nāʻiwi family and to use them as guideposts. On a smaller scale, it was easier to remember the place names along Waioli stream in Hanalei if you could link these places to a romantic story of a young man's search for the woman of his dreams.

Some of the stories are designed to explain local phenomena, such as the reason for Waimea river sometimes flowing red, or why the Mānā beaches are dangerous for swimmers.

The stories, however, are intended to amuse and entertain, not to carry a heavy historical significance. Enjoy them.

GLOSSARY

'ahē-ke'oke'o   a dry land taro (which means it does not have to grow in water) indigenous to Kauai. It had a whitish corm and base that were small and tough to eat, and light green leaves that had a white spot where the leaf blade came from the petiole.

'ahē-'ula'ula   an indigenous dry land taro of Kauai that had reddish shadings on the corms and leaves, ranging from faint flecks to distinct maroon coloring. It, like the white variety, grew wild in the uplands.

ahi-lele   "leaping fire," the name given to the fireworks cliffs on Kauai, one at Hā'ena, the other at Nu'alolo.

'Aiko'o   a wind at Nu'alolo. Its name means "canoe-eating."

'ākala   *Rubus hawaiiensis,* a wild raspberry.

'ākepa   a member of the honeycreepers (*Loxops coccinea caeruleirostris*) that eats insects. They fly in flocks with short quick movements. They are olive-green on top, with yellow beneath, and have brown wings and tails.

akua   any supernatural being, from gods to ghosts.

'alae   *Gallinula chloropus sandwicensis,* the Hawaiian gallinule, or mudhen, who had the secret of fire before Maui forced them to give the secret to him so he could pass it on to mankind.

'alae   *Asplenium horridum,* a fern that grows up to 3 feet high. It was also called 'iwa. The stems have dark brown hairs and scales, and were used to make hats. From the names associated with it, this small tree fern reminded the viewer of a bird.

Alaka'i   the great swamp at Kōke'e. The name means "to lead," since a traveler through the swamp must be led by a guide, for one false step can take one into a bottomless pit of water and mud.

'alani   any tree of the species *Pelea,* of which mokihana is the best known member.

'alani-wai   a shrub (*Pelea waialealae*), cousin to the mokihana and found only in the highest, wettest parts of Kauai.

Alapi'i   the bottom of a ridge at Nu'alolo where a rope ladder was located. The name means, simply, "The way up."

ānuenue	the rainbow.
Ānuenue	a goddess, sister of the great gods Kāne and Kanaloa. Her visible sign was the rainbow and her descendants of high chiefly rank were known by the rainbow hovering near them.
ʻauwai	an irrigation ditch that brought water to taro patches.
auwē	a word that expresses wonder, surprise, fear, pity, or affection, depending on its inflection.
ʻawa	*Piper methysticum,* a shrub 4-to-12 feet in height; also, the narcotic drink made from its root.
Hāʻena	the area from Wainiha to the beginning of Nā-pali, formerly only sandy plains and dunes. The name literally means "red hot." *Hā* means to dance accompanied by song; *ʻena* means raging like a fire, wild, untamed, so the name Hāʻena may have something to do with the hula school, a reference to a wild, untamed dance?
hala	the pandanus tree, *Pandanus odoratissimus,* one of the endemic trees of Hawaiʻi. Its leaves were woven into mats, hats, and baskets. The flowers were used to scent tapa. The red fruit sections were used for leis and for brushes to paint designs on tapa.
Hale-leʻa	"joyful house," a side valley that opens into Wainiha.
hale moe	"the sleeping house," a special structure used only for sleeping, one of at least six to be found in any compound, others being used for eating, storage, and so on.
Hanakāpīʻai	one of the small valleys in Nā-pali region, Hāʻena side of Kalalau.
Hanakoa	one of the valleys in the Nā-pali region.
Hanalei	"the bay in the shape of a wreath," the name given to the bay and valley considered the most beautiful in Hawaiʻi.
Hanapēpē	one of the great valleys that sweep from the mountains to the shore on the southwestern side of Kauai. The name is translated as "crushed bay."
hau	*Hibiscus tiliaceus,* a tree that grows along the seacoast, especially where its roots are watered by streams. The wood is soft.
heʻe	general name given to any squid or octopus.
heʻe mākoko	*Polypus ornatus,* a variety of octopus having an ornamentation of large, red spots. It lives in the deep ocean and has a bitter taste. It was eaten only in times of famine.

heiau	a place of worship, ranging from a simple enclosure to an elaborate, walled, stone-floored area containing many houses, altars, and wooden sculptures of the gods.
He-wahine-manawa-leʻa	"the woman who is generous in giving alms." She and her husband offered hospitality to the Piliwale sisters in Kalalau and so were spared.
Hiki-mauna-lei	Nā-iwi's daughter, whose name means "wreath that comes from the mountains."
hinahina	*Heliotropium anomalum,* a low, spreading beach plant whose vine-like tendrils were used as cordage.
Hina-ke-kaʻā	the beautiful and shy aunt of Maui. Her name can be broken down thusly: *Hina* is short for Hinahele, goddess of the fishes; *ke* means "the"; and *kaʻa* is the string that fastens a fishhook to the line.
hōʻiʻo	a wild fern, *Deplazium arnottii,* whose fiddleheads are good to eat raw or cooked and taste like very young asparagus.
hōʻiole	similar to a rat, rat-like.
Holoholo-kū	the third of the seven heiau along the Wailua River. This is thought to be the oldest heiau on the island, and is where high chiefesses came to give birth to their children. It was also apparently used as a place of refuge; hence its name "Run-Stand."
hōlua	the name given to especially prepared sliding platforms. There is one in Waimea Canyon and another in the uplands of Kōloa.
Hōlua-manu	"slide of Manu." The remnants of this slide can still be seen on the Ka-lehua-hakihaki ridge in Waimea Canyon. The peak of the ridge, which is 3,724 feet high, is named Ka-holua-mano on present day maps.
hula	the overall term for music and dance. The hula school at Hāʻena trained students in the religious songs and dances. The schooling lasted seven years.
huli	"offspring." Banana plants send up offshoots from their roots which can be dug up and replanted.
iho-lena	a variety of banana with small, salmon-pink fruit that was one of the few kinds of bananas that women were permitted to eat.
ʻiʻiwi	*Vestiaria coccinea,* a red feathered bird with a long curved beak that lives in the upland forests. Their feathers were used in the cloaks,

capes, and leis that are Hawai'i's greatest art. The bird was caught, a few feathers plucked, and released again to grow back its lost feathers for another time.

imu	the oven dug in the ground and lined with volcanic rock and heated by fire. When the rocks are glowing red, food is placed in the oven with them and covered over. Actually the food is steamed, not baked.
Ka-āhole	a small valley south of Nu'alolo.
Ka-hala	"the pū hala tree."
Ka-hala-māpuana	"the fragrant hala tree," a place on the banks of Waioli Stream, Hanalei. *Māpuana* also means a wind-blown fragrance, which lends this area a more poetic aura.
Ka-hale-lehua	"the House of Lehua," the name of a demi-goddess who lived in the upper Wailua region.
Ka-hauna	"the Stink," the original name for the Dry Cave of Hā'ena.
Ka-he'e-hauna-wela	one of the manifestations of the god Kanaloa, translated to mean "the evil-smelling squid."
Kahiki	usually translated as any foreign place, or the lands and islands to the south, especially Tahiti.
Kahua-nui	the sister of Lohiau and Limaloa. Her name means "Great Foundation." She was the head of the hula school at Hā'ena and high chiefess of the district which was always ruled by a woman and totally independent politically from the rest of the island.
Ka-'ulu	the breadfruit tree.
kahuna	the general name for the priests who also acted as doctors, soothsayers, and the like.
kahuna kilokilo	the priest whose duty it was to study the sky, stars, and clouds for omens of present and future events.
Ka-iki-hauna-kā	"the little rotten-smelling vine," a place name for Kukui heiau which is located right on the sea. This area, on modern maps, is called Alakukui, which means "the way to Kukui."
Kala-lau	a valley in the Nā-pali area, once heavily populated. The name means "leaf of the 'ākala berry," the 'ākala being a member of the raspberry family native to Kauai.

Ka-lau-heʻe	"the squid sheet," a spot in a little stream that flows into the Wainiha River where tapa, left to soak for any length of time, rots and becomes slimy, looking and feeling something like a squid.
Ka-leleʻa-lu-aka	"the image of a dripping sea creature," the name Ka-ʻōpele gave his son, which is apt considering what Ka-ʻōpele must have looked like after a six-month sleep in the ocean depths.
kalili	*Viola kauaiensis,* a violet endemic to Kauai that grows in the high boggy areas of the mountains.
kalukalu	a member of the sedge family, a rush or grass growing in wet places. It was used to make string and grew only at Kapaʻa.
Ka-maile	"the maile vine," name of a chiefess who gave her name to one of the two fireworks cliffs on Kauai.
Ka-moʻo-kōlea-ka	"the lizard who professes immediate friendship without the least meaning it sincerely." That is the name of a ridge that starts just behind the town of Hanalei and rises towards Nā-molokama.
Kāmū	"silent," after one of the two groups of Mū people who inhabited Kauai even before the Menehune came. They lived in the far reaches of valleys and remained silent, not calling attention to themselves.
Kanaka-nunui-moe	*Kanaka* means "man," *nunui* means "very large," and *moe* means "sleepy"; therefore, the name means "sleeping giant."
Kanaka-pīpine	"Stingy man." Stinginess was held in great contempt in the olden days.
Kanaloa-huluhulu	"hairy giant," the giant who, looking for his head, tore up the grassy area in Kōkeʻe where the park headquarters now are.
Kāne	one of the four supreme gods of Hawaiian religion. He is the god of natural phenomenon and is thought to be the first of the gods to arrive in Hawaiʻi. His voice is heard in the thunder. Many rocks were set up in his honor.
Kāne-ʻalohi	"sparkling man," uncle of Lau-haka.
Ka-nē-loa	"the permanent lack" (or "deprivation"). This name appears often in Hawaiian stories, and usually the man so named is a loner, a man always seeking a home or a place in a chief's retinue. Even if he finds it, he doesn't keep it for long.
Ka-ʻōpele	"the one protected by taboo." ʻŌpele was the name of the patron of fish who lived in Waiʻanae on Oʻahu.

Ka-pa'a	a small district in Kawaihau. The name seems to mean "The Solid (place)," in opposition to the ocean or the sky.
Kaua-hoa	"companion in war," a solitary warrior, friend of Lima-loa. There are several men of this name in Kauai stories.
Kauai	the name of the fourth largest island of the Hawaiian archipelago. As a child I frequently heard the name pronounced to rhyme with "cow eye" and sometimes pronounced in three soft syllables "kau a i," but never with the explosive glotteral heard today that makes Kauai rhyme with Hawai'i. I heard Kauai story tellers imitating a country bumpkin's speech by including excessive and explosive glotterals. The language variation spoken on Kauai had few glotterals and used the "t" sound instead of "k," which is kept in such words as "tapa" and "ti."
ka-ua-lau	a spotted banana. Its name means "many rain drops."
Ka-uka-'opua	a place far up the Waioli stream. *Uka* means "inland," "towards the mountain," and *'opua* means "puffy clouds." This was undoubtedly a place where the clouds or fog built up near the foot of the Nā-molo-kama waterfall.
Ka'ula	a small island 22 miles southwest of Ni'ihau.
Kāmaulele	a peak in the Līhu'e region of Kauai.
Ka-'ū-maka	"The Sorrowful Eye." This is on the point between Wainiha and Hā'ena.
Ka-wai-hau	a great land division of Kauai, with the Wailua River in its center. The name may be translated as "the cool water," from the fact that the area is well watered by streams flowing from the highlands.
Ka-wai-kini	"the abundant water," the highest point on the island of Kauai.
kawelo	the name of a species of fish, as well as a variety of sweet potato. There was a famous warrior of Kauai named Kawelo, but he belongs to a later period than the legends told here.
Kawelo-lani	the name of a star that rises low on the horizon in the month of October only. It was accompanied by another star named Kau-ka-malama.
kawelo-kupa	a variety of sweet potato that grows in the mountains.
kāwelowelo	to wave, flutter, or whip in the wind as a flag does.
Ke-ala-hula	"the way to the hula school," an indication to where the trail went. It is the ridge between Waikoko and Lumaha'i.

Kē'ē	the beach and point at Hā'ena at the start of Nā-pali. Here was the most noted hula school in Hawai'i. The name may be from the concept of criticism, especially from a hula critic. Kē'ē was the name given to the hula master who was invited by another hula master to criticize his class.
keiki	a child.
Ke-kāne-lokomaika'i	"the man with good intestines." The old timers believed the feeling of generosity arose in the small intestines; therefore, this name means "the generous man." He and his wife were hospitable to the Piliwale sisters when they visited Kalalau.
Ke-li'i-koa	the chief of Kawaihau whose life was made miserable by a magical coconut tree. His name means "the brave chief."
ke pele	a choice tapa (made on Kauai) which was dyed gray with a charcoal of burnt sugar cane mixed with coconut water. It was scented with maile.
kīhei	a rectangular piece of tapa worn as a cloak by tying two ends in a knot over one shoulder.
Kī-lau-ea	a land area east of Hanalei on the north coast of the island.
Kilohana	"lookout point," the place high in the mountains that has a fantastic view down into Wainiha, Lumaha'i, and Hanalei valleys, whenever the clouds permit.
kilo pōhaku	a flat, smooth stone that was placed in a bowl of water and that acted somewhat like a crystal ball, in that omens would be seen reflected on the rock in visual pictures.
kō	*Saccharum officinarum,* the sugar cane, one of the most valuable members of the grass family.
koa	*Acacia koa,* a tall tree having reddish, hard wood, bearing crescent moon-shaped leaves. Its silvery green color and spreading canopy and usefulness are often mentioned in Kauai stories.
koai'e	*Acacia koaia,* a tree related to the koa, but smaller. The wood is harder than the koa and was used for spears, paddles, and fine tapa beaters.
Koai'e	the name of the largest secondary canyon within the Waimea Canyon complex, undoubtedly named after the trees which must have grown abundantly there before they were cut down to supply the whaling ships' needs. *Koai'e* also became an uncomplimentary word, somewhat like our "country bumpkin."

koali	any member of the morning-glory family, *Ipomoea spp.*
koili	to rest on something as lightly as the moon rests on the surface of the sea or a butterfly on a flower.
kō-kea	"white sugar cane," one of the varieties known in ancient days.
Kōke'e	an area along the top edge of Waimea Canyon, whose name means "to wind about or bend," probably because the trail winds about to avoid the canyon.
kolohe	mischieveous, naughty, with an element of amusement on the part of the trickster. Also to behave in this way.
Kō-mali'u	"well-seasoned sugar cane"; figuratively, having a deep skill or profound knowledge in sugar cane.
Ko'olau-wahine	the morning wind that blew over the Mānā plains. She was thought to be mischievous but not dangerous as she hurried into the Ko'olau hills.
Ku-a	Nā'iwi's son. The name is shortened from Ku-a-pōhaku, "to turn to stone."
kukui	*Aleurites moluccana,* one of the most useful and beautiful trees native to Hawaii. Its nuts were used for food, decoration, and oil for burning.
Kukui	a heiau on the seashore north of the Wailua River on the point named Lae Alakukui. The walls facing the sea were 16-to-22 feet across and contain some tremendous stones. Note that this heiau is named both in the story of Kanaka-nunui-moe and Ka-'ōpele.
Kulu-'i-ua	"swift great rain," the name of the young chief who fell in love with the woman of the rainbow.
kupa	a native of a place.
Kū-pā-kō-'ili	possibly "standing fence of sugar cane"; the name given to a grove of 'ōhi'a-'ai. There was a variety of sugar cane that had a deep red cane with green stripes. The sugar cane was named from the 'ōhi'a-'ai tree.
Kūpono-aloha	"faithful love," the man who became the second husband of Kamaile.
kupua	a semi-divine being that could assume several physical forms and usually had some magical power. See Niu-lōlō-hiki and Kawelo-o-Mānā.
La'ahana	Maikoha's daughter, the goddess who taught the art of marking patterns on the beaters, which gave a watermark effect on the finished tapa.

Lā‘au	forest; the seventh village in Wainiha Valley, the farthest upstream.
lama-kū	"standing torch." For a description, see Ma-ka-ihu-wa‘a.
Lani-huli	"curling over the sky," a romantic name for an ox-bow where the river appears to double back on itself like a breaking wave. This is the third place name from the mouth of Waioli Stream.
Lau-haka	*lau* is a thatched mountain hut as used by birdcatchers, and *haka* means "to roost, as chickens do," so the name of this birdcatcher who became a chief of Waimea for a time may be translated as "Roosting Hut."
lau-hala	the leaf of the hala tree, used for making baskets and mats.
Lauhuki	Maikoha's daughter; the goddess who gave and taught skill and wisdom to expert tapa makers.
laukona	a variety of sugar cane, having green and yellow striped leaves.
lehua	a tree, *Metrosideros macropus,* that is one of the most beautiful on Kauai. It has bright, feathery flowers, usually red, and is a favorite food of the ‘i‘iwi, the red-breasted honey creeper. Symbolically, the lehua stands for all aspects of love between man and woman.
lei	a wreath of flowers, berries, or leaves, which can either be left open or closed into a circle. It is worn around the shoulders or around the head.
Lima-loa	a famous warrior of Kauai, brother of Lohiau. He often was seen striding through his village, dressed in a feather cape and carrying his war club—in the mirage that was often seen at Mānā before the swampy land was filled in to grow sugar cane.
limu	a general name for seaweeds of all species.
Lohiau	a chief that lived at Hā‘ena and became first the husband of the fire goddess Pele, then of her sister Hi‘iaka. His sister was Kahua-nui; his brother was Limaloa whose image appeared in the mirages of Mānā.
lo‘i	prepared taro patches, having stone walls covered with earth and having a means of being irrigated with fresh-flowing water.
loli	a sea slug, *Holothuria spp.,* that is spotted and rather ugly to look at. It was used as food in time of famine. The heat of the hand can melt it.
loli-mākoko	a species of sea cucumber speckled with red dots.
lua	a form of hand-to-hand combat that used all the techniques of wrestling and boxing, except that its aim was to maim, dislocate joints, and break bones.

Lua-muʻu	the ancestor of both the Mū and Menehune peoples. The Menehune were considered "human" while the Mū were thought of as "wild."
Luehu	the huge elongated fish or eel whose humps became the islands of Hawaiʻi.
Luma-haʻi	a wild and sparsely settled valley. *Luma* means "to kill someone by putting his head under water." *Haʻi* is the name of a particular form of gathering dead bodies slain in war, as an offering or sacrifice. Luma-haʻi had a great quicksand area where robbers disposed of travelers and their horses, burying forever all evidence of their crime. Do these ideas go together?
Māeaea	"stench," a beach near Waialua on Oʻahu.
Māhā-mōkū	crab-netting. *Māhā* is a net with a mesh large enough to take four fingers at a time. *Mōkū* is a method of catching crabs by baiting a net so the crab crawls along the net and entangles its feet. This is the name of the area at the mouth of the Waioli Stream.
Māhie	"pleasant." It is a place in the Kōkeʻe region.
Maikoha	the god of tapa makers. When he died, the first paper mulberry trees grew from his grave. He had instructed his daughters in the use of this plant and they became goddesses of tapa making, from planting to finished product.
maile	a vine, *Alyxia olivaeformis,* that grows in the high forests. Its leaves keep their fragrance even when dried. In myths, it is often symbolic of a faithful love, probably because it entwines itself in trees.
Ma-ka-ihu-waʻa	"at the canoe's prow," a ridge that starts on the west of Waioli stream and mounts to blend into the massive mountains behind.
Makana	"gift," the name of the fireworks cliff at Hāʻena. At its base is the upper wet cave, first dug by Pele when she sought a home on Kauai.
Mākua-iki	a ridge along one side of Nuʻalolo Valley.
malo	a thin strip of tapa worn by men. It circled the waist and looped between the legs.
māmaki	a tree growing up to 15 feet high that bears tasteless white mulberry-like fruit (*Pipturus albidus*). Its bark gave a coarse heavy tapa which was strong when dry but tore easily when wet.
māmane	*Sophora chrysophyllia,* a native tree that grows either as a sprawling mass near the ground, or as an erect tree up to 40 feet high.

Its wood is very hard and durable and so was used for heavy wear items like sled runners and farmers' shovels.

Mānā	the long, sandy plain on the southwest side of Kauai that stretches between Kekaha and the start of Nā-pali. In the old days, this was a marshy place and famous for its mirages.
Manini-holo	a Menehune fisherman at the time of the leaving. His name was given to the Dry Cave at Hā'ena, and means "running sturgeon," an apt name for a fisherman.
Manō	a name frequently given to a man. It means literally a shark, but figuratively it means a chaser after women, a wolf or Don Juan type.
Mānoa	the valley and stream that is on the east side of the Dry Cave at Hā'ena. Its name is said to mean "to thicken," but how that applies to this place is anyone's guess.
ma'o-hau-hele	*Hibiscus brackenridgei,* a three-foot tall shrub bearing bright yellow flowers. It is a native of Kauai; its name means "green traveling hibiscus." Do I scent another story here?
manu	the generic name for bird; a common male name.
Manu'a-kepa	a place along the Waioli Stream; its name can be translated as "accumulated-burrs," a place where grasses grow a burr-like seed.
Maui	the most famous demi-god of Hawai'i, who gave fire to mankind, slowed down the sun, and attempted to join the islands into one continent. Also the name of the second largest island of the Hawaiian chain.
Mauna-hina	"gray mountain"; name of the stream that flows from Kilohana into Wainiha Valley. Another nearby stream bears the name of "black cliff."
mele	a song or a chant, frequently used for made-up stories, as opposed to strict history or genealogical chants.
Menehune	one of three small peoples who lived on Kauai, by some accounts being there before the Hawaiians came. They had great strength and engineering knowledge. They worked cooperatively as a group and were unwilling to finish any project not completed in one night.
milo	a tree, *Thespesia populnea,* that resembles the hau, and was used to make calabashes and other implements.
Milu	the land of the dead, located in the ocean depths off Polihale heiau at Mānā.

mokihana	a small tree that grows only on Kauai, bearing berries that smell of anise. The berries were used for their scent, as even the driest of them keep fragrant for years.
Momo-iki	a surfing place near the mouth of the Wailua River. Exactly where it is and what the name means is lost.
Mono-lau	"fruitful-leaf," the name given to the area where a spit of sand comes into the bay at the mouth of Waioli Stream.
mū	*Monotaxsis grandoculis,* a fish, perhaps a porgy or snapper.
Mū	a race of people who are perhaps the original settlers of Kauai. They used the banana plant for food, clothing, and for all their woven goods.
Nā-hale-maile	the wise grandmother who gives Nā-lei-maile the maile wreaths and axe that he used to cut down the magical coconut tree, Niu-lōlō-hiki. The name means "the maile houses."
Nā-hiku	"the seven," the name given to the Big Dipper constellation, which in Hawaii dips into the ocean.
Nā-holoholo	"those that run," the name given to Venus, a planet that runs about the sky as opposed to the fixed stars.
Nā-'iwi	"the 'i'iwi birds," the Mū father who lost his wife and two children to the sun.
Nā-lei-maile	"the maile wreaths," the young man who succeeds in cutting down the coconut tree, Niu-lōlō-hiki.
Nā-molo-kama	"the twisting children," the name of the great waterfall that drops into Hanalei Valley. In times of heavy rains as many as 23 different cascades fall down beside this permanent waterfall.
nanau	unfriendly, crabbed, sour, bitter; paying no attention to a call; to ignore, as former friends.
Nā-pali	the area between Kē'ē beach at Hā'ena and the beach at Polihale, full of cliffs and steep valleys.
Nā Piliwale	four sisters who are associated with famine, and with the class of people who associated themselves with a chief but performed nothing useful to the group. When the food and hospitality ran out in one place, they moved to another.
naupaka	a shrub, *Scaevola,* that has half flowers. Some species grow at the shore, some in the mountains. It is said that when the two half-

flowers are brought together, they form a whole. There are two legends concerning the origin of naupaka on Kauai.

Niu-lōlō–hiki   the surviving brother of Maui who took the form of a coconut tree. The name means "the coconut that can act stupidly," which goes along with his behavior in the story. Another coconut tree goes by the name Niu-ola–hiki and has the same power to elongate itself.

noni   a small evergreen tree or shrub, member of the coffee family (*Morinda citrifolia*). Its leaves are thick and dark, shiny green. It has strange fruits that look somewhat like small breadfruit. The bark gives a red dye and the root gives a yellow dye. Both leaves and fruit are used as a poultice which is applied to sprains, bruises, and broken bones to aid in their healing. In times of famine, the fruit can be eaten, but one would have to be really hungry.

Nou   "thrower," the name of the boy who threw fire-brands from Makana.

Nu'alolo   a valley in the Nā-pali region of Kauai, famed for its fireworks cliff and hanging rope ladder. *Nu'a* was the name given to the hog sacrificed upon the completion of a canoe. *Lolo* was the name for the religious ceremony at which the brain of the sacrificial animal was eaten.

'ōhi'a-'ai   the mountain apple, *Eugenia malaccensis,* that bears edible and delicious red and white fruit. Too much of the fresh fruit, however, acts as a powerful laxative.

'ōhi'a-hā   *Eugenia sandwicensis;* like the mountain apple, but having red fruit.

'ōhi'a-lehua   *Metrosideros macropus,* another name for the lehua tree that bears brilliant red feathery flowers.

'Ō'ili-kū-ka-heana   the chief who brought 'awa to Kauai from Kahiki. His name means "that sort of bumpy skin like that of a corpse of one killed in battle," a reference to the 'awa-induced quality of his skin.

'ōlena   *Curcuma domestica,* the tumeric.

olonā   *Touchardia latifolia,* a shrub whose bark was twisted into cord used for fishing nets and a basis for feather work.

'Ōma'o   a valley in the Waimea Canyon, whose name means green.

O'o-a'a   the sister of Pōhaku-o-Kane and Pōhaku-loa. Her name means "fast-rooted." In the 1946 tsunami, she moved into the sea. Divers can see her in the depths as she waits for her brothers to join her.

'ōpae	generally the name for any shrimp, but mostly refers to the fresh-water shrimp found in upland streams hiding under rocks.
'Ōpae-wela	a stream in the Waimea Canyon complex that flows into Waimaka stream, and is on the south side of Hōlua-manu. The name means "hot shrimp."
'opihi	a sea limpet that grows on the rocks of a reef; one of the *Helconiscus* family.
pahipahi	a children's game similar to "peas-porridge hot," involving the rhyth-mic slapping of hands accompanied by singing.
pala'ā	*Sphenomeris chusana,* the lace fern.
palapalai	a three to four foot fern, native to Hawai'i. Its stem is pliant enough to make excellent wreaths.
pana 'iole	a boy's game. Rats were put into a pit and boys shot at them with bows and arrows.
papa hōlua	the sled used on the hōlua, or sledding platform. It was very long and very narrow. The greatest sliders could stand on it like a surfer, but most sliders were content to get down the course lying on their sleds.
Pele	goddess of the volcano. She searched Kauai for a home but failed to find one and moved on to Hawai'i.
Pihana-ka-lani	"gathering place of high supernatural beings." It was the name of the fifth heiau from the mouth of the Wailua River. There were seven heiau in all.
pīkoi	a wooden dagger about 22 inches long, with a rounded grip and a blade which had a concave curve ending in a sharp point. It was car-ried with a wrist loop.
pili	*Heteropogon contortus,* a tall grass that was used for thatching roofs and walls of houses.
pili-mai	a yellowish green variety of sugar cane, often used in love potions.
pili wale	to be emaciated because of famine; also to live carelessly without thought of the future, e.g., eat everything without putting some by; and also to live off a chief without giving anything in return.
Piliwale-haluhalu	one of the four Piliwale sisters. Haluhalu means 1) to be thin as a person poor in flesh; 2) to be hungry for food; 3) to be greedy after what is another's.

Piliwale-kualana-ka-ōpū	one of the four Piliwale sisters. Her name says that she is very hungry, lazy, indolent and bored, and roves about without a chief to support her.
pō	"night." The world was created from the chaos of pō and brought into ao, the dawn.
Pōhaku-loa	the brother of Pōhaku-o-Kāne and Oʻo-aʻa. His name means "Long Stone." Today he lies beside the road, completely covered with vines. Several times county workers have wanted to move him away, but each time they have left him in peace.
Pohaku-o-Kāne	"stone of Kāne." Many large, specially shaped rocks were considered blessed by the god Kāne. Offerings of flowers, leaves, or food are still left to them. Kāne was the god of natural phenomena.
poi	taro that has been boiled and pounded into a paste, slightly sour to taste. After the taro has been pounded, but before water is added, poi will keep for a long time.
Poli-hale	the four-terraced temple at the western end of Mānā built on the steep slope that begins the Nā-pali region. In the ocean depths below Poli-hale was the land where the dead dwelt.
poni	a variety of taro that turns a deep purple when cooked.
pōpō-ʻulu	a banana with a short green trunk that women were permitted to eat. Its taste is reminiscent of breadfruit.
pū hala	the screw pine (*Pandanus odoratissimus*). Its spirals of saw-toothed leaves and innumerable aerial roots seem, even more than the coconut, to be the symbol of the tropics. Guides love to tease tourists by claiming the pū hala fruit is really a pineapple.
Puna	another name for the district of Kawaihau. *Puna* refers to a spring of water, and so the area may be named according to the plentiful supply of water.
tapa (kapa)	the cloth made from beating strips of mulberry bark together. The sheets were then decorated, one of ancient Hawaiʻi's art forms. Fragrant leaves, like maile and mokihana, were frequently beaten in to give a scent. Tapa was whitened by washing it in the ocean and spreading it out on the beach to dry.

ti (kī)	a plant, *Cordyline terminalus,* which is one of the most useful even to-day. The leaves are used as decoration, as plates, hula skirts, brooms, or woven into sandals. The roots are a source of sweetening and are used in making kūlolo, a mixture of ti and taro baked.
ua	the term for any water falling from clouds; the rain. Hawaiians, keen nature watchers, distinguished between different kinds of rainfall: long, short, misting, and so on.
ʻuala	*Ipomoea battatas,* the sweet potato vine. There were many species recognized by the Hawaiians. It seems to have been introduced about the same time as the breadfruit tree, later than the first settlers.
Ua-lena	"yellow rain," the name of a yellow-tinted rain that falls at Hanalei.
ʻukiʻuki	a species of lily (*Dianella*). It bore dark blue berries that were crushed to make a blue dye. The leaves were used to thatch house walls.
ulua	an adult jack fish, *Caranx,* about five feet long, weighing over a hundred pounds, and of excellent eating quality, raw or cooked.
ʻuwaʻu	*Pterodroma phaeopygia sandwichensis,* the dark-rumped petrel, today an endangered species.
Wai-ʻalae	a mountain, stream, and waterfall in the Waimea Canyon complex. The name means "mudhen-water," perhaps because the mudhens were plentiful there.
Wai-ʻaleʻale	the highest mountain on Kauai. Its name means "rippling water," because on the average more rain falls here than anywhere else on earth.
Wai-aloha	a spring at Hāʻena, between Mānoa and Limahuli streams. The name means "loving water." The water is particularly good tasting.
Wai-a-lua	"twin waters," a land division on Oʻahu.
Wai-ʻamaʻo	"green-water," a place name near the source of Waioli Stream in Hanalei. Undoubtedly a place where water flowed over mossy rocks.
Wai-ʻanae	"mullet-water," a land division on Oʻahu.
Wai-koko	the stream farthest west in Hanalei Valley, whose name means "bloody water."
wai-lele	"leaping water," a waterfall or cascade.
Wai-lenalena	"yellow water." It is the name of a small valley near the top of Wai-ʻaleʻale. It is remarkable for the huge-leafed hāhā plants found there.